DUNGEONS &
DETECTIVES

HARDY BOYS ADVENTURES

#19 *DUNGEONS & DETECTIVES*

FRANKLIN W. DIXON

ALADDIN New York London Toronto Sydney New Delhi

ALADDIN

An imprint of Simon & Schuster Children's Publishing Division

1230 Avenue of the Americas, New York, NY 10020

First Aladdin paperback edition October 2019

Text copyright © 2019 by Simon & Schuster, Inc.

Cover illustration copyright © 2019 by Kevin Keele

THE HARDY BOYS MYSTERY SERIES, HARDY BOYS ADVENTURES,

and related logos are trademarks of Simon & Schuster, Inc.

Also available in an Aladdin hardcover edition.

All rights reserved, including the right of reproduction in whole or in part in any form.

ALADDIN and related logo are registered trademarks of Simon & Schuster, Inc.

For information about special discounts for bulk purchases, please contact Simon & Schuster Special Sales at 1-866-506-1949 or business@simonandschuster.com.

The Simon & Schuster Speakers Bureau can bring authors to your live event.

For more information or to book an event contact the Simon & Schuster Speakers Bureau at 1-866-248-3049 or visit our website at www.simonspeakers.com.

Series designed by Karin Paprocki

Interior designed by Mike Rosamilia

The text of this book was set in Adobe Carlson Pro.

Manufactured in the United States of America 0919 OFF

2 4 6 8 10 9 7 5 3 1

Library of Congress Cataloging-in-Publication Data

Names: Dixon, Franklin W., author

Title: Dungeons and detectives / by Franklin W. Dixon.

Description: First Aladdin hardcover/paperback edition. | New York : Aladdin, [2019] | Series: Hardy boys adventures ; #19 | Summary: Frank and Joe Hardy search a mysterious castle for clues to a stolen, extremely valuable comic book.

Identifiers: LCCN 2018059332 (print) | LCCN 2018061201 (eBook) | ISBN 9781534421073 (eBook) | ISBN 9781534421066 (hc) | ISBN 9781534421059 (pbk.)

Subjects: | CYAC: Lost and found possessions—Fiction. | Comic books, strips, etc.—Fiction. | Castles—Fiction. | Brothers—Fiction. | Mystery and detective stories.

Classification: LCC PZ7.D644 (eBook) | LCC PZ7.D644 Dun 2019 (print) | DDC [Fic]—dc23

LC record available at https://lccn.loc.gov/2018059332

CONTENTS

LET THE GAMES BEGIN

1

FRANK

I **STUMBLED BACKWARD, MY GRIP ON THE SWORD** tightening as I parried the blow from the attacker's blade. I tried to block out the sounds of martial combat raging around us and brace myself for her next attack. The leather armor I was wearing wasn't going to do much good if the curved blade of her saber penetrated my defenses. I'd already been wounded once in the battle. One more strike, and my quest was over for good.

"Drop your cutlass and surrender, peasant," Xephyr spat, her eyes smoldering beneath her black cowl. "Or your life will be mine along with the treasure."

"Never!" I sneered, trying to sound more intimidating than I felt. "You and your henchmen will never get your hands on the queen's jewels!"

This wasn't the first time I'd handled a sword, but my opponent fought with the skill of a fencing champion. Which was exactly what Xephyr (with an *X*) was.

They say the best defense is a good offense. I didn't know if that was true, but an attack of my own might catch her off guard and give me a desperately needed advantage. As I went to lunge, the sun glinted off the metal-spiked cuffs on Xephyr's arms, temporarily blinding me. I hesitated. Xephyr didn't. Her blade found its mark. The sword fell from my hands and I collapsed to my knees.

"Noooo!" Joe yelled, sprinting across the field to avenge my death.

I dusted myself off and walked across the Bayport Memorial Park baseball diamond to the dugout bench, where the rest of the deceased were sitting.

"I bet I'm the first reporter to cover a magical medieval battle on a baseball field," Charlene Vale said from a crouch as she snapped photos of the action with her DSLR camera. "These LARPing pics are going to look great on the front page of the *Bayport High News* website."

"Some of us do a better job of putting the 'live' in live-action role-play than others," I joked, sliding my realistically painted foam sword into the dugout's bat rack.

"Nice quote, Hardy," Charlene said, putting down her camera and picking up the little notebook she carried around everywhere.

I hoped she couldn't see me blush. My last girlfriend,

Jones, had left Bayport after her mom got a job out of town, and Charlene had been the first new girl to catch my eye. Or, maybe I should say "re-catch." She was our school's top student journalist, and I'd kinda had a crush on her for a while, so I was secretly super excited that she wanted to feature me in her article on Bayport's fantasy-role-playing culture.

"You did better than me," my friend Murph said, his rubber elf ears wiggling. "Robert stabbed me twice before I got to cast a single fireball spell."

Two total hits from either a foam weapon or a beanbag "spell" and you were "dead." Normally, a teammate could tap you to bring you back to life after a few minutes, but this was the final sudden-death match before Sir Robert's Comic Kingdom opened and we took the role-playing inside, swapping our swords for dice.

Eponymous comic shop owner Robert McGalliard was the only adult member of the Bayport Adventurers Guild LARP club. Inside his shop, he was just a big, lumbering middle-aged man with a bald noggin and a passion for comics. Out here with a sword in his hand, he danced across the battlefield with the grace of a deadly ballerina. Only instead of a tutu, he wore a traditional Scottish kilt that he claimed had been passed down from an ancestor who fought in the First War of Scottish Independence—although it was always a bit hard to tell what was and wasn't true when it came to Robert's boasts.

Robert and Xephyr fought toward each other, dropping their opponents like flies. Dennis "DM Dennis" Dovan was the last of Xephyr's henchmen to fall. Joe followed, another victim of Xephyr's sword. Soon Robert and Xephyr were the only two warriors standing.

"No offense, but you guys really stink at this compared to them," Charlene said, snapping away with her camera from the dugout.

"No offense taken," Dennis said cheerily, good-natured as always.

"Yeah," I mumbled under my breath. I was going to have to find another way to dazzle Charlene besides LARPing prowess. She could be pretty intense, especially when it came to reporting a story, and we'd been classmates long enough that I knew impressing her wasn't easy.

I didn't take the barb personally, though. This really was about as epic as a foam weapon battle could get. With both Robert and Xephyr in costume, you almost forgot it was make-believe.

Robert finally pierced Xephyr's defenses, tapping her on the heart with the tip of his foam sword. Xephyr didn't break character for a second. She let out a gut-wrenching scream and clutched the end of the sword to her chest as if it were embedded there for real.

"Curse you, Sir Robert," she muttered before collapsing to the ground. "Revenge . . . shall . . . be . . ."

Her body shuddered and went still.

"Sir Robert the Exaltedly Wonderful is victorious yet again!" Robert raised his sword over his head and shouted in his distinctive Scottish brogue. "Now to the shop!"

"Huzzah!" nearly everyone yelled in unison, raising their weapons in the air and following Robert in a magical medieval procession across the park toward the comic shop. The only ones who didn't "huzzah!" with rest of us were Charlene and Joe.

"How come you're not in costume?" Charlene asked my brother.

"I'm here for the live-action part," he said, twirling his foam sword. "I'm too cool for the role-playing."

"Ha!" I laughed. "Too closed-minded is more like it."

"I think a detective like you would really dig the tabletop role-playing games we play at the shop if you gave them a chance, Joe," DM Dennis said, referring to Joe's and my reputations as Bayport's foremost teenage private investigators. "You have to use all kinds of investigative problem-solving skills in RPGs like Sabers and Serpents."

"Yeah, and the action kicks butt!" Xephyr added, thumping the hilt of her sword against her breastplate and walking ahead of us to the front of the procession. "I'm gonna go show Robert pics of my costume from last night's LARP camping trip."

Xephyr had made the realistic faux saber herself, along with most of the other foam weapons we'd used for the LARP. They were so impressive, Robert even sold them at the comic shop. She made costume armor too, and the outfits for her LARP characters were always great.

"You guys sure do take your role-playing seriously,"

Charlene commented, watching Xephyr strut off. "These are all characters from the Sabers and Serpents games you play at Comic Kingdom?"

"Yup! Games like S and S let you create a fantasy character with their own personality, skills, weaknesses, and special powers and then think your way through situations like they would," Dennis explained enthusiastically.

"You can be a whole other person. Or even another creature!" I said, giving one of Murph's elf ears a friendly flick.

"In tabletop games, dice play a critical role too," DM Dennis chimed back in with a wink, pulling a gleaming silver polyhedral twenty-sided die from his pocket. "For every major choice a character makes, whether it's sweet-talking an ornery wizard or firing an arrow at an orc, you have to roll one or more dice to see what the outcome is."

Dennis held up the number 20, known in the gaming world as a critical hit. "We call this die the D20, and the die don't lie. Roll high enough and you can succeed spectacularly. Roll too low"—he turned the die to the digit 1, the dreaded critical fail—"and it could mean your life."

"The DM in 'DM Dennis' stands for dungeon master," I informed Charlene. "He runs all the games we play."

"The term 'dungeon master' comes from Dungeons and Dragons, but I'm the game master for other classic RPGs like Sabers and Serpents as well," Dennis said.

"We'd call him GM Dennis, but it doesn't quite have the same ring to it," Murph pointed out.

"LARPing in our S and S characters followed by a table-top campaign has been our new Sunday morning tradition since Rob moved to Bayport and opened the shop a few months ago," I said as the shiny new sign for Sir Robert's Comic Kingdom came into view down the street.

"I did some digging after Robert contacted me to pitch the article on the Adventurers Guild and Sabers and Serpents," Charlene said. "It doesn't seem like many people except vintage collectors knew about the game until he opened shop and started reviving it."

"Not even many people in Bayport knew about it, and it was created right here!" Murph asserted.

"You're interviewing the right guy, Charlene," I said, patting Murph on the shoulder. "We don't call him Murph 'the Collector' Murphy for nothing."

"S and S has always been legendary in collecting circles for its artwork and how rare the material is, so naturally I knew all about it," Murph said proudly. "The game was an early competitor to Dungeons and Dragons way back in the 1970s, but a warehouse fire put them out of business before it really took off. Kids today wouldn't be playing it at all if Robert hadn't uploaded the old rules manual to the Comic Kingdom website."

"It's the local-interest angle my readers really want to know about. Rob's uncle Angus was one of the creators, but I couldn't find a single interview with him anywhere," Charlene said.

"I thought Robert just moved here from Scotland," Joe interjected.

"He did, but his uncle emigrated years ago," Murph said. "A huge part of the game is based on their family's ancestral castle on the outskirts of town."

"Wait, Robert's uncle is Old Man McG?!" Joe asked incredulously.

"The one and only," I confirmed. Joe usually only came by on Sundays for the fighting and hadn't paid much attention to the shop until now.

Old Man McGalliard was a notorious curmudgeonly hermit who was rumored to throw rotten apples at any kids—and shoot at any adults—who crossed Castle McGalliard's moat. And, yes, it had a moat! A crumbling, very-badly-in-need-of-repair moat, but still, how many small American towns have a real eighteenth-century castle? It was an exact replica of a medieval Scottish castle, and according to Robert, the walls were still decorated with the same ancient weapons the original owner, a McGalliard ancestor who had left Scotland for the American colonies, had put up over two hundred years ago. From what I knew of local history, no one had lived there or bothered to take care of it for generations until Robert's uncle moved back to claim it.

Castle McGalliard's heir apparent paused in front of the comic shop, turning to face everyone before unlocking the door.

"Hurry up, you dawdlers, and gather round," Robert

called. "As I promised our young reporter friend, I have a special announcement to make before commencing the day's indoor adventures." He paused so the rest of us could catch up before continuing. "As most of you are aware, I am the proud owner of one of the world's rarest comic books."

"Yeah, we're aware, you only brag about it about twenty-five times a day," Xephyr quipped.

"As would you, my fearsome lass," Robert replied, grinning. "The pristine copy of *Sabers and Serpents #1* hanging in the impregnable, bulletproof glass case behind my counter is one of only three copies in existence. And the *only* one that's completely intact."

He took a deep breath and a dramatic pause, as he liked to do when telling his favorite story.

"Many people today think of Sabers and Serpents as just a role-playing game. Which it was at first, and thanks to its revival here at Sir Robert's Comic Kingdom, it still is," Robert continued. "But my uncle and his partner, Filmore, had also been preparing to launch a comic book tie-in to promote the game in 1976."

"You know that fire we talked about?" Murph asked Charlene. "Well, there was never an issue number two, because Filmore Johnson burned down the printer's warehouse with everything in it right before number one was released. No one ever found out why."

Charlene's eyes lit up. "Readers love a good local scandal."

"It's not just local," Murph said. "Filmore was a

super-popular comic book artist nationwide before he helped start Sabers and Serpents, and he vanished without a trace right after the fire."

"It wasn't just Filmore that disappeared either," Robert said. "The only other copies of the comic to surface after the fire inexplicably have the same exact page ripped out. Rumors about its contents have swirled for decades."

"The whole incident is one of the greatest unsolved mysteries in comics and gaming history," Murph said reverently. "That's part of why the comic is so valuable."

"Indeed," Robert said. "And of the three copies left in existence, mine is the *only* copy containing the legendary missing page."

"Not that you've ever shown it to us," Murph complained. He'd been trying to get Rob to open the case ever since the shop opened.

"And for good reason, my lad," he replied. "As everyone can tell by the cover, it's in unprecedented fine condition. A mere fingerprint, or heaven forbid, a tear, could reduce the comic's value by thousands."

"He's got a point, Murph," Dennis said.

"Until now, my crabby old uncle Angus, Filmore Johnson, and I have been the only souls to ever know what that page contains. Filmore hasn't been heard from, and Uncle Angus hasn't left the castle or given an interview since *Sabers and Serpents* went belly-up in a ball of flames over forty years ago."

"So if I got your uncle to talk on the record, it would be a worldwide exclusive?" Charlene asked seriously.

"Ha! You're about as likely to get an interview with Nessie the Loch Ness Monster," Robert scoffed. "I can barely get the old codger to say hello to me when I come in the castle door, and that's after I've bribed him with a bar of chocolate."

"Collectors and gamers have been trying for years," Murph concurred sadly.

"But our family's silence over the missing page is about to come to an end," Rob declared, pausing to look down at his watch. "Five days from now, at midnight on All Hallows' Eve, when I reveal it to the world in a livestream from the castle during the grandest Halloween masquerade party this town has ever seen."

Just about everyone erupted at once.

"Yes!" Murph shouted.

"No way!" exclaimed Dennis.

"Sweet!" Xephyr cheered.

"Woo-hoo!" I joined in.

"I've got the perfect costume!" Joe declared.

"Robert's about to unveil one of the collecting world's holy grails and you're thinking about your Halloween costume?" Murph asked in disbelief.

"How often do you get to dress up for a Halloween party at an actual castle?" replied Joe.

"Invitations with the news are scheduled to go out to the

world right"—Robert paused as a handful of phones buzzed and beeped with a new alert—"now."

"What prompted you to disclose the missing page at this time?" Charlene questioned Robert, pen at the ready.

"There will be a special guest in attendance at my costume soiree," he answered. "Wendell Leadbetter, a top appraiser from none other than Butterby Auctioneers, called me asking to examine *Sabers and Serpents #1*. He will be present at the soiree to confirm the authenticity of the comic and appraise its undoubtedly spectacular value."

"Butterby's is one of the premier auction houses in the world," Murph informed us. "They sold the last copy of the S and S comic for more than fifty thousand dollars, even with the most important page missing. The comic and gaming worlds have been waiting forty years to see what's on that page. *If* the copy is in the excellent condition Robert claims it is, then it would be worth a fortune."

"Ye have little faith, my young friend," Robert said. "All shall be revealed in a few days' time. Now let's enter the kingdom and gaze upon the glory that is *Sabers and Serpents #1*."

With a comic of that value on the wall behind the shop's counter, Robert didn't seem to take any chances with security. Anybody who spent much time around the shop heard him brag about how expensive his security system was. Not only did the front door have a giant dead bolt, he had to enter a keypad code *and* press his thumb to a fancy, state-of-the-art biometric fingerprint reader to deactivate the alarm system. You could see the security camera—one of many he had set up around the shop—blinking from behind the glass above us as the door clicked open.

Robert pushed his way confidently through the comic shop door, flicked on the lights, and instantly froze in his tracks.

"NOOOOOO!" he and Murph both screamed at the same time.

The impregnable glass case that protected *Sabers & Serpents #1* was gone.

MISSING IN ACTION

2

JOE

I'VE BEEN ROBBED!" ROB WAILED, DROPPING to his knees.

"Time to ditch the sabers and break out our magnifying glasses, bro," I said to Frank as everyone stared at the empty wall behind the counter, where the prized comic was supposed to be. I may not have been that into role-playing games, but solving crimes was right up my alley. "It looks like one of the gaming world's biggest unsolved mysteries just became our latest case."

"You guys really use magnifying glasses to investigate crimes?" Xephyr asked. "I thought that was just in old detective novels."

"Metaphorical magnifying glasses," I replied, stepping toward the counter to examine the wall. There were a bunch of less valuable collectible comics displayed in smaller protective cases on either side, but all that was left from *Sabers &* *Serpents #1* was a dusty rectangle where the glass case had been. That and a pair of holes in the plaster where the screws had been ripped from the wall.

"Everybody else step back," Frank said to the group. "We don't want to contaminate the crime scene."

Charlene promptly ignored him, pushing her way forward as she clicked away with her camera.

"I mean, uh, everybody else," Frank mumbled.

I shook my head. My brother tends to get a little tongue-tied when he has a crush.

"This article keeps getting better and better," said Charlene.

"Now I'll never get to see the missing page," Murph moaned.

Robert sounded like he was trying to say something, but all that came out were whimpers.

"Wow, somebody must have critted their sleight-of-hand check to break in here with all this security," Dennis observed nonsensically.

"Was that English?" I asked.

"In RPGs like S and S, you have to roll skill checks with the D20 to perform different actions," Frank explained. "Sleight of hand is the skill a rogue or a burglar might use to pick a lock. A 'crit' means a critical hit."

"Well, no one touch anything, in case this rogue of yours

got sloppy," I said. "The police will want to dust for prints."

"No police!" Robert finally managed to blurt.

Frank, Charlene, and I each gave him the same curious look.

"I, um, well, let's just say I didn't always have the best experience with local law enforcement back home in Edinburgh," he sort of explained. "I'd just rather handle it privately, and you boys are practically better than the police anyway. Everyone talks about the Hardy boys and all the cases you've solved. You can get the comic back for me, can't you? You have to! Please! Before the party!"

I looked at Frank. Robert's nervousness about the police was a little suspicious, but we did have a long history of beating the Bayport PD to the chase. Chief Olaf might not be happy about it, but . . .

"We'll do our best," Frank told him.

"Not if I beat you to the scoop," Charlene said.

"Maybe we can work together to solve the case," Frank said hopefully, but Charlene already had her sights on Robert.

"How did they get in and what else was taken?" she demanded.

She could have been nicer to my bro, but I had to hand it to her, she had good investigative instincts.

Charlene's question must have triggered alarm bells in Robert's head, because his mouth dropped open and he sprinted for the door marked PRIVATE at the back of the shop. He emerged a moment later and quickly opened the cash register, revealing a drawer full of tidy, entirely un-stolen bills. He sank down in the chair with a dejected sigh.

"The back-door lock is broken, but they left the register and the safe untouched," he said. "Not that it matters much. It's all pennies compared to that comic."

"Doesn't look like anything is gone from the shop, either," Xephyr commented, giving a look around.

"Were you working last night?" I asked her. I'd been around the shop enough to know that Xephyr helped out behind the counter part-time.

"Nah, Rob worked the late shift. Dennis and I were at the big annual LARP camping trip over in Bayport Heights," Xephyr answered.

"Awesome costumes, by the way, guys," said Frank. "The live updates everyone posted online were great, especially the pics of Xephyr's werebear."

Charlene and I both cleared our throats at the same time. Leave it to my brother to nerd out about a costume in the middle of a crime scene.

"What? They were really cool," Frank said defensively.

"Speaking of pictures," I said, pointing at the security camera over the counter and changing the subject back to the crime at hand. "Why didn't the alarm go off when they broke in the back door?"

"Oh, well, um, that is curious . . . ," Robert mumbled.

"Let's check the security footage and see just how good this burglar's sleight of hand was," Frank said.

Robert suddenly turned a shade paler, then leaped up and pointed toward the front door. "Out! Everybody but my detectives out! The shop is closed until further notice."

There were grumbles from Murph and the rest of the LARPers, but Robert marched out from behind the counter and forcibly shoved everyone out the door.

Everyone but Charlene. She hadn't budged.

"The footage," she demanded.

"Yes, well, I'm not sure it's really necessary to check the video," Robert fumbled.

"Dude, someone just stole your prized super-valuable comic book right in front of your security camera. Of course it's necessary," I said.

"Unless there's something you don't want us to see." Charlene said what we'd all been thinking.

"Off the record?" Robert asked her.

"As long as I still get the exclusive on the theft," she said.

Robert sank back into his chair. "You won't find anything on the tapes."

You could practically feel three sets of teenage eyebrows rise at the same time.

"The cameras aren't hooked up. None of it is. It's all for show," he admitted. "I never paid to have any of it turned on."

LAW AND DISORDER

3

FRANK

UT WHAT ABOUT ALL THOSE TIMES you bragged to everyone about how expensive and high-tech your security system is?" I asked Robert, who was suddenly too busy fiddling with his hands to look me in the eye.

"Must keep up appearances, you know," he said. "Talk the walk, as it were."

The shop door jingled behind us before I had chance to ask him what else he'd been lying about.

"Got a call about a theft," a familiar voice said as I turned around to find Bayport's top cop, Chief Olaf, standing in the doorway.

"Hi, Chief!" Joe chirped with a grin. "Nice costume."

"Costume?" the chief replied. "What are you talking about, Hardy? This is my uniform."

"And a handsome uniform it is, sir," Joe said enigmatically. I had a feeling my brother had something up his sleeve. I just wasn't sure what it was yet.

Chief Olaf eyed Joe and me suspiciously.

"Hello, officer," Robert greeted Chief Olaf nervously. "No need for you to trifle with such a small matter as ours. I'm sure you have more important police business to attend to."

"A small matter?" the chief asked, staring at the conspicuously blank rectangle where the case on the wall behind the counter had been. "You and I must have a different definition of that phrase, because the caller said the thief took a comic worth more than fifty grand."

Robert scrunched his eyes shut and groaned, as if the number had punched him in the stomach. "More than that, actually, but I wouldn't want to worry you with my troubles. I've already hired an investigative service. Save the taxpayers some money, you know?"

Chief Olaf looked from Joe to me and growled, "Investigative service my rear. How many times do I have to tell you boys to stay out of police business?"

"It's probably been about three hundred so far, so maybe three hundred and one?" Joe asked innocently.

"Out!" shouted Olaf, holding the door open with one hand and pointing with the other.

"Care to make an official statement about the theft, Chief?" Charlene asked, holding up a small digital recorder as Joe and I made our reluctant exit.

The chief sighed. "You again. You're almost as troublesome as these two. If you want a quote, you can call the station after the report is filed. Now I want everyone except the proprietor out of my crime scene."

"Let the professionals handle this," he told Robert as Charlene followed us out the door. "A theft of this magnitude isn't for amateurs."

I could see Robert squirming in his chair. We were going to have to finish our conversation later. His nervousness about the police was more than a little shady, and I wondered what else he wasn't telling us.

I turned to Charlene to ask her if she wanted to pool our resources and partner up to solve the case together, but she was already halfway down the block, cell phone to her ear. I sighed. I had a hunch she was a lot more interested in being the first to break the story than being part of the team.

"Sorry, bro," Joe said sympathetically. "I think she's only got eyes for the scoop."

"You guys are gonna find it, right?" I heard Murph ask meekly.

I looked down to see him still sitting on the curb, with one of his elf ears missing, looking forlorn.

"I don't know who's more broken up about this, Robert or you," Joe said.

"I've been dying to see that missing page since Comic Kingdom opened," said Murph. "Being the first to witness something like that unveiled is a collector's dream. Not to mention all the online speculation that the missing page might contain clues to Filmore's disappearance." Murph looked around furtively and lowered his voice. "And maybe even real treasure."

"Let's walk and talk," Joe said. "I want to know more about this comic."

Murph hopped up to follow us. Like I'd told Charlene, Murph hadn't gotten the nickname "the Collector" by accident. Collecting wasn't just a hobby for him, it was an obsession. From games to comics to Japanese toy robots to dinosaur fossils, if it could be collected, there was a good chance he either collected it or knew a ton about it. His expertise had come in handy on cases before, and his mastery of comics and gaming history made him more of an expert than possibly even Robert.

"Okay, Murph, I've seen the rest of the comic from the pictures the other owners have posted online too. I agree that the story line suggests that the missing page is a treasure map," I said. "But even if it is, it's still part of a make-believe story. It's just a rumor that it could lead to actual treasure. It may drive up the comic's value, but there's no evidence to back it up."

"What if Angus and Filmore just wanted you to think it was a make-believe story?" Murph asked cryptically.

"Um, doesn't this game have wizards and magical monsters?" Joe asked dismissively. "Sounds pretty make-believe to me."

"What if the fantasy is a smoke screen?" asked Murph, undeterred by our skepticism. "Everyone knows that Angus used Castle McGalliard and real artifacts he found there as the inspiration for the game, right?"

I nodded. Filmore's illustration of the castle was even on the comic's cover in the background, behind a sword-wielding knight entwined in the coils of a nasty-looking sea serpent.

"Okay, so I always had a feeling there might really be something to the legend of the treasure because of that. Then one day I was flipping back through my old Butterby catalogs," Murph began.

"You read auction catalogs?" Joe asked.

"Of course. Doesn't everybody?" Murph replied earnestly. "They're highly collectible. I have a whole library of them. Anyway, so I discovered that the last copy of *S and S #1* Butterby's sold was part of a local estate sale. It didn't have the treasure map, obviously, but it did show up in an old trunk full of miscellaneous stuff found by a lifelong Dumpster diver from Bayport. There's no way to tell where or when the guy found everything, but it looked like this guy was a frequent visitor of Filmore's neighborhood trash cans. I'm guessing he came across the trunk when Filmore's place was cleaned out after he disappeared. There were a few crumpled sketches from an earlier comic book Filmore had illustrated and an engraved watch with his initials, but most of the stuff besides the comic was auctioned off for next to nothing."

"If there's still no map and the rest of the stuff was worthless, then what's the big deal?" asked Joe.

"I didn't say it was worthless," Murph corrected with a sly grin. "I just think I'm the only one who saw the value. No one else seemed to make the connection to Sabers and Serpents, but there was also a beat-up eighteenth-century shipping ledger written in Gaelic bearing the initials *PMG*. Well, I did a little digging into the town records, and Paul Magnus McGalliard happens to be the original owner of Castle McGalliard."

"So you think the ledger belonged to Robert and Angus's first American ancestor?" I asked.

"Not only that, I think Angus and Filmore used it to come up with part of the story for the comic."

Murph pulled out his phone, flipped to his bookmarked photos, and pulled up a picture of the open ledger from the auction catalog.

"Hey, I recognize those words!" I exclaimed, examining a familiar series of cryptic words made of archaic letters and accents that looked kind of similar to the English alphabet, but were impossible for me to understand. I turned to Joe. "See those strange letters? They're written in Gaelic, an ancient language that was native to Scotland. Some of those Gaelic words appear in both the game and the comic."

"They sure do," Murph concurred. "The entire ledger is written in Gaelic, but thanks to the magic of the Internet, I was able to translate a lot of it into English. From what I can tell, it isn't just an innocent merchant's shipping ledger, it's a *smuggler's* ledger. The ledger is dated 1774. That was still colonial times, right after the Boston Tea Party, and it looks like ol' PM McG was hiding goods he didn't want to pay taxes on to the English government."

"Whoa, if that's true, then it's an amazing artifact from Bayport's early history," I observed.

"Some of it also uses a pretty basic code, but it wasn't hard to decipher," Murph continued eagerly. "From what I can tell, some of the made-up Gaelic words that appear in the game are really code words taken from the ledger. Most of these code words stand for everyday goods like fabric, spices, and tea. But can you tell which one is different from the rest?"

I examined the picture and scanned my memory for the words I recognized from the game.

"Each of them shows up in the comic except that one," I said, pointing to an unintelligible three-letter word.

"Exactly," said Murph with a twinkle in his eye. "Makes you wonder why only that one is left out of the comic and where else it might appear. Especially when you decode it. Because that's the one that stands for gold. In the ledger that code word appears in an entry cataloging eight crates of gold."

Joe and I went silent as we processed what Murph had just told us.

"You think Angus and Filmore took the Gaelic words in the comic from Angus's ancestor's smuggling ledger—" I began.

"And the missing page could be a map with the code word for gold on it?" Joe jumped in to finish the question.

"Not just the word," Murph said. "I don't know if Angus and Filmore realized the significance of the ledger they found, and no one but them and Robert know what was on that missing page—"

Joe cut him off before he could finish.

"But what if one of those things was clues to a smuggler's stash of real gold?"

4

INK STAINS

JOE

WHOA, SO THIS COULD BE A CLUE to a real-life treasure hunt?" I asked. I was developing a deeper appreciation for role-playing games, that was for sure.

"In the ledger, the sentence above the word for gold translates to 'Beneath the windmill I lay awaiting, a drop in the bucket and a chain afar,'" Murph said. "What if there's a windmill on that map that marks the spot where it's buried?"

"Could be, but we've still got the more immediate mystery of who stole the comic to solve first if we ever want to find out," Frank reminded us. "And a fifty-thousand-dollar-plus price tag is a big enough treasure to start with."

"What's our suspect list look like?" I asked. "The comic

was displayed front and center in the shop, and Sir Robert isn't the most discreet guy in the world, so I'm guessing plenty of people knew about it."

"It definitely wasn't a secret," said Frank. "He boasted about it pretty much constantly."

"Not just in person, either," Murph said. "He was all over social media and comic forums, blabbing about it to promote Comic Kingdom's website."

"Well, 'the entire Internet' is a pretty big suspect pool, so let's narrow it down," I suggested. "Do you guys know if Robert had any enemies? Or maybe someone who'd expressed an unusual interest in the comic recently?"

"It wasn't me!" Murph exclaimed, and Frank and I both laughed.

"Besides you, Murph," Frank assured him. "We should probably talk to this Wendell Leadbetter fellow from Butterby Auctioneers. Robert probably won't want us spilling the beans about the theft, but it's bound to get back to them, and it's possible Butterby's recent interest is somehow connected."

"So what do you know about this Leadbetter guy, Murph?" I asked.

"Oh, I mean, nothing really, just that he works at Butterby's is all," Murph replied. "But I do have an idea about one of Rob's enemies. Inkpen's Ink Pen has taken a real hit since Rob showed up in town, and word is Don Inkpen isn't all that happy about it."

"The rival comic shop owner across town—that makes sense," Frank said.

"DM Dennis used to run his games out of there before Comic Kingdom opened up, so Rob stole Inkpen's top game master along with a lot of his comics business," said Murph.

"Okay, so we've got two leads to start with," I said.

Murph's phone buzzed.

"Gotta go, guys. There's an online auction for some rare gubernatorial campaign buttons from the 1960s that's about to end. You'll let me know as soon as you find out anything?"

Frank nodded and typed something into the search bar on his phone. Then he looked up at Murph and said, "And you let us know if you think of any other leads."

Murph nodded in return and hustled down the street, his lone elf ear wiggling elfishly. Frank had his phone to his regular-person ear immediately.

"Hello, Mr. Leadbetter, my name is Frank Hardy and I'm calling regarding Robert McGalliard's copy of *Sabers and Serpents #1*. Please call me back as soon as you get this. It's urgent," Frank said into the phone, then left his number and clicked off.

"That leaves Inkpen," I said.

Inkpen's Ink Pen didn't look that different from Sir Robert's Comic Kingdom. Racks and bins full of comics, glass cases full of collectible toys and figurines, and shelves full of games, with tables set up in the back for kids to play their favorite RPGs on-site. The one thing there was less of?

People.

Aside from three kids at one of the game tables, the only person there was a guy with close-cropped hair and huge muttonchop sideburns behind the counter, reading a vintage Black Panther comic book. He had a tattoo of Wonder Woman on one arm, Chewbacca on the other, and a T-shirt with Wolverine arm-wrestling Captain Kirk from the old *Star Trek* TV series.

He grinned slyly when he saw us walk in the door and tossed the comic onto the counter.

"Haven't seen ya in a while, Franky," he said in a deep Rhode Island accent, a New England dialect I recognized from other cases. I'm definitely not a linguistics expert, but to me it sounded a little like Boston meets Brooklyn. "Guessing you ain't here for the new *Detective Comics*. From what I'm hearing on the grapevine, you're looking for something a little rarer."

"You wouldn't happen to have a copy of *Sabers and Serpents #1* in stock, would you, Don?" Frank played along. "I had my eye on one at a shop across town, but someone grabbed it before I saved up enough allowance."

"Funny thing, I just got one in today. Hundred and five K, and it's yours," Dave Inkpen said deadpan, then burst out laughing. "You don't really think I broke into that loudmouth's store, do you? Not that I wouldn't shake the hand of whoever did. If you catch 'em, let 'em know they've got ten percent off their next purchase at the Ink Pen."

"That's real generous of you," I said, looking around the nearly empty shop. Of the three "customers" gaming in the back, I recognized one of them as Inkpen's son Doug. "Doesn't take superpowers to tell your business is down, or that you've got a bone or two to pick with Robert. Some folks might call that a motive."

Inkpen glared in my direction. "Between him and me, if anyone's a thief, it's McGalliard. I've had the corner on Bayport's comic market for near on twenty years, and that oaf thinks he can sail right into my town and steal my business for himself just because he's lucky enough to be related to Old Man McG." He slammed his fist on the counter, causing a Squirrel Girl bobblehead to topple over. "Heck, if I knew how to pull a heist like that and thought I could get away with it, I mighta even thought about it. But what am I gonna do with a hot comic that rare? There are only three in existence. Someone slipped it under my shop door, I couldn't even sell it if I wanted to. The only thing that rag could buy me is a trip behind bars, and I don't plan on spending my golden years behind nothin' but this here counter."

"What about the black market?" Frank asked. "I'm sure someone as savvy as you could find a buyer if they really wanted."

He snickered. "You think that highly of me? It's flattering, but you been reading too many comic books, kid. You think I

31

got the names of rich foreign princes in my Rolodex who I can move that thing to? If I had those kinds of friends, I wouldn't be struggling to pay the Ink Pen's rent. A guy would have to have some serious Bruce Wayne/James Bond–type top secret connections to pull off that kind of deal. That comic shows up anywhere outside of the dark web, the Batcave, or some evil mastermind's lair, and everyone and their grandma gonna know exactly where it came from."

It was obvious Don Inkpen had it in for Robert, but he also made a lot of sense. Why would someone steal a comic they couldn't possibly get away with selling?

Inkpen scratched his left muttonchop pensively. "Come to think of it, I know of one fella might profit from that comic being stolen."

Two sets of Hardy boy ears instantly perked up.

"And he's big, bald, and Scottish."

Two sets of Hardy eyes fixed Don Inkpen with a dubious glare. Sure, Robert had been acting sketchy, and it was clear his relationship with the truth was a bit shaky, but . . .

"What motive could Robert possibly have for stealing his own prized comic?" Frank asked skeptically.

"If that thing's in the condition McGalliard says it is, it's gotta be insured for a fortune," said Inkpen. "And if it gets stolen, the insurance company ain't gonna take no twenty-five percent commission off the top like the auction house would neither. A fella who maybe ain't as well off as he says he is could make out pretty on a loss like that."

GOING, GOING, GONE

5

FRANK

JOE AND I STOOD ACROSS THE STREET a few minutes later, staring back at the shop as two of the three kids who'd been playing tabletop games in the back filed out, leaving Don Inkpen and his son Doug alone in their now empty Ink Pen. Doug was a couple of years older and used to LARP and play RPGs with us, but he'd stayed loyal to his dad's shop. He'd been in some of the pics from the big LARP camping trip out in Bayport Heights, so I guessed he stayed in touch with some of the gang. I'd barely seen him in person, though, since Comic Kingdom opened. Doug was a nice guy, and I felt bad about him being left out, but he wasn't the Inkpen I was concerned with. It was what his dad said that had my brain churning with questions.

Could the Ink Pen's grumpy owner be right about his boisterous crosstown rival? Was it possible that Robert had staged the theft himself to collect the insurance money?

"Robert did lie about his security system," Joe said, reading my thoughts. "Maybe he's just cheap and didn't want to spend the money. Or maybe—"

"Inkpen is right and he doesn't have the money," I finished Joe's thought.

"If he knew the cameras weren't on, it means he also knew there wouldn't be any footage to implicate him. As the shop's owner, Robert had the means and opportunity to take the comic if he'd wanted," Joe said, referencing two of the three basic defining characteristics of a viable criminal suspect—the ability to commit the crime and the chance to pull it off. That still left the third and most important factor.

"I'm not sold on the motive, though," I said. "And I think you were right about Inkpen having a motive himself. He doesn't hide his feelings about Robert."

"Motive, definitely, but means and opportunity are questionable," Joe pointed out. "Even if he could pull it off, he's right that it doesn't make sense to steal something you can't easily profit from."

"Unless his primary objective was to hurt Robert's business and reclaim some of his customers," I countered. "There's more than one way to profit from the theft."

"Trying to shift the suspicion back onto Robert would be a clever way to help cover his tracks, too," Joe observed.

"So why would Robert make his own comic disappear right before he was planning to have it appraised in front of everyone?" I pondered.

"Especially if there was the chance that it could sell at auction for as much as Murph seems to think," Joe agreed.

"Auctions are risky, though," I said, playing devil's advocate. "You have no control over who bids, and there's always the chance it could sell for less. I know Murph's taken losses on some of the collectibles he's put up for auction online."

"Yeah, but swiping your own prized attraction right after announcing its unveiling to the whole world is a pretty wacky party promotion tactic," Joe said. "It makes him look like a chump in front of the entire world, and for someone as fond of bragging as Sir Robert, that's gotta sting."

My pocket buzzed. I pulled out my phone and saw the words *Butterby Auctioneers* flash across the screen.

"Frank Hardy here," I said, putting the phone on speaker so Joe could listen in.

"Yes, this is Wendell Leadbetter of Butterby's returning your call," answered a man with an upper-crust British accent. "You mentioned something about a copy of *Sabers and Serpents #1*?"

"Thanks for calling me back so quickly, Mr. Leadbetter. I'm a private investigator helping out Robert McGalliard. I'm not sure if you've heard the news yet, but I need to discuss your upcoming trip to Bayport on Halloween to appraise his comic."

"My trip to Bayport? I'm not sure I follow. Are you offering to sell a copy of *Sabers and Serpents* for the McGalliard family? I'd certainly be interested if so, but I'm in Japan appraising Edo period artwork for the next week and half. I'm afraid I can't make it back to the States for an appraisal until early next month."

I exchanged a confused look with Joe. "I'm sorry, Mr. Leadbetter, I think maybe I'm the one who doesn't follow. I thought you'd already made plans with Robert to appraise the comic this Friday."

He gave an amused chuckle. "I'm quite sure I would have remembered that. It's not every day I get to examine a comic as rare as that one."

"You never contacted Angus McGalliard's nephew, Robert?" I asked, although I already had a good idea about his answer.

"I'm afraid it appears someone has played a practical joke on both of us, Mr. Hardy," he replied.

Twenty minutes later we were back on the other side of town, marching toward Comic Kingdom's front door. But Robert wasn't on duty, just Xephyr.

"Sir Rob's rather discombobulated by the whole bloody ordeal," she told us, using the made-up accent of her Sabers & Serpents character. Xephyr might be the most into role-playing; she liked to pretend to be one of her characters, even when we weren't playing. "He took the rest of the afternoon off after the authorities departed. He said not to disturb him unless the stolen item reappeared or aliens invaded. He's gotta come in tomorrow, though, because we've got school," she said, switching back to her normal voice. "I want to help the poor guy out, but it's not like I can skip class. Besides, I don't want to miss fencing practice."

I tried calling his phone anyway, but it went straight to voice mail.

"Looks like we're going to have to come back tomorrow as soon as school lets out," I told Joe.

Either Robert was lying, or—

"I—You—He—It—How—What?" Robert uttered, stumbling over his words along with his feet as he collapsed back into his chair when we confronted him after school the next day. "You mean I've been conned?"

"Or you're the one doing the conning," Joe retorted. "We haven't made up our minds which yet."

Robert buried his face in his hands, massaging his cheeks and his forehead like they were a mound of stubborn clay. He'd shooed the rest of his customers out of the shop and flipped over the CLOSED sign as soon as he'd seen the looks on our faces when we walked in the door, so we were alone in the shop.

"You're saying Wendell Leadbetter isn't really Wendell Leadbetter?" he whimpered.

"Oh, Wendell Leadbetter is Wendell Leadbetter, all right, but whoever you say called you about that appraisal isn't him," said Joe.

"But I spoke to him myself on the telephone," he moaned. "Surely there's some mistake. He even sent me a contract for the appraisal!"

"Can we see it?" I asked.

"It's back at the castle with the rest of my paperwork," Robert said, looking even more distressed than when he'd discovered the comic missing. "But it's got 'Butterby Auctioneers of London' right there on the top in fancy gold-foil print, and Wendell Leadbetter's signature on the bottom, notarized with an official stamp! There's even a British stamp on the envelope! It must be real! It must!"

"Easy enough to forge if someone knows what they're doing," I informed him. "Did you verify his identity when he called you?"

"I . . . I looked him up on the Internet. Does that count?" Robert asked hopefully. "His name was right there on Butterby's website!"

"Anyone could have done the same thing and used his name," Joe said. "Did he give you a phone number?"

Robert pulled a folded piece of paper from his wallet and laid it on the counter with shaking hands.

"It's a London exchange, but it has a different area code from Butterby's," I observed.

"He said it was his cell phone," Robert croaked.

Joe dialed. We could all hear the automated voice that answered.

"The number you have called is temporarily out of service."

"I don't know whether it's us or you, but someone has definitely been played," Joe said.

Robert just moaned.

I'd LARPed with the big guy enough to know he was a decent actor, but his distress certainly seemed genuine. He opened and closed his mouth a couple of times like a fish, but no actual words came out until the third or fourth try.

"There's . . . there's no one coming from Butterby's to appraise my comic once you find it?" he asked meekly, the reality of the con apparently finally sinking in. We both shook our heads.

"So, assuming you're the duped and not the duper, there's a good chance whoever did the duping could have pinched the comic as well," I speculated.

"Sure seems like there's a link, but I don't see how the dots connect," Joe said. "What would the thief gain by pretending to be an auction appraiser and then stealing the comic before the appraisal?"

"Gain . . . ," Robert repeated bitterly, muttering to himself as if in a stupor. "Ha! Looks like the joke's on me. Ha-ha. Didn't see that one coming."

Then he started to giggle. Or cry. It was kind of hard to tell.

"Um, are you okay, dude?" Joe asked.

"Fine! Right as rainbows!" Robert declared, standing up abruptly. "Things happen. Life is challenging. But you forge ahead. Keep calm and carry on, as they said in the Second

World War. Onward and upward! Now out you go, lads. You've done your best. Some cases just can't be solved."

"Wait a second, we still don't know who took the comic," Joe said as Robert tried to usher us to the door.

"No need to worry yourselves anymore with my misfortunes," he insisted. "The local constables can take it from here, I'm sure."

"But I thought you didn't trust the police," I tried reminding him.

"Oh, I don't know. That Olaf seems like a fine fellow. And he did give me a rather stern talking-to about aiding and abetting the delinquency of minors. Wouldn't want to get on the wrong side of the authorities, now would we?"

Robert gently pushed us out the door. "And don't forget the Halloween party! Tell your friends. Tell your neighbors. Still have a business to promote, you know. The show must go on!"

"Hold on a second . . . ," I protested.

Robert didn't.

"Toodles!" He pulled the door shut behind us and locked it. The shop lights flicked off a moment later for good measure.

Joe turned to me as I watched Robert's lumbering silhouette retreat through the glass.

"Um, did we just get fired?"

BLAST FROM THE PAST

6

JOE

WELL, THAT WAS MORE THAN A WEE bit suspicious," Frank said as we trudged back toward the car. "He almost seemed more upset about the appraisal being a hoax than having the comic stolen. Without a comic to appraise, what does it matter?"

"I think the poor guy might be cracking up," I commented. "Hearing he'd been robbed and conned all in the same day might have pushed him over the edge."

"So are we really dropping the case?" Frank asked.

"It would make Chief Olaf happy, that's for sure," I said. "Which is a pretty good reason to keep investigating, if you ask me."

What fun was it making the chief's life easier?

"And it would let Murph down. He's emotionally invested in finding that comic too," Frank asserted.

"Well, that's two good reasons to keep going," I said.

And keep going we did, though we didn't make much progress in the few hours left before we had to be home to finish our homework for school the next day.

At school on Tuesday, we interviewed all the kids who hung out at the shop, but no one had any useful info. Everyone just wanted to know what we'd found out so far. We kept the revelation about the auction appraisal hoax to ourselves, though, along with the fact that we'd technically been dismissed from the investigation.

We were committed to solving the case, whether Robert wanted us to or not. We just didn't have much to show for our stick-to-itiveness yet. Frank and I rehashed everything for, like, the twentieth time as we walked to the car after school. I'd parked off campus so we could avoid the usual after-school parking-lot traffic jam.

"So basically, we're stumped," I concluded, hopping into the car and starting the engine.

I looked in the rearview mirror, put it in reverse to back out of the parking space, and—

POP-POP!

Frank and I jolted in our seats as both rear tires blew at once.

"Whoa, what did you just hit?" asked Frank, shaking off the shock of it.

We hopped out of the car to inspect the damage. What we found were two totally flat tires and a bunch of small metal doodads that looked like rusty old spiked jacks. There was also a note pinned to the left tire by one of the spikes.

We both looked around to make sure whoever had put those spikes down wasn't still lurking, but, as far we could tell, the street was empty.

Frank pulled the note from the tire and read it aloud. "'Back off, or the next thing to get pierced won't be your tires.'"

My brother and I shared a determined look. Any lingering question about whether we were dropping the case had just been answered. If someone thought they could intimidate Joe and Frank Hardy off an investigation, they didn't know the Hardy boys.

Frank leaned down and picked up one of the spikes to examine it. It was made of two small iron tines twisted with four nasty barbs in place of the usual blunt ends. The way it was designed, no matter how it landed, two of the spikes would always be pointing up, primed to pierce anything unlucky enough to either roll over or—I winced at the thought—step on it.

"Caltrops," Frank said. "My Sabers and Serpents character carries a set in his explorer's pack. They were originally designed as a type of ancient antipersonnel weapon combatants would leave on the ground to take out unsuspecting enemies or their animals when they stepped on them. They were common in medieval European warfare."

"How old are those things?" I wondered, gently taking the caltrop from Frank and touching one of the rusty points. "They look like real-deal antiques from the Middle Ages."

Frank's eyes suddenly lit up. "Hmm, I can think of at least one place in Bayport someone might be able to get their hands on real medieval weapons."

I smiled. The caltrops had us down two tires, but up one lead. "Wouldn't be the town's only replica of a medieval Scottish castle, would it?"

LUCK OF THE DRAW

7

FRANK

WAITING FOR THE CAR TO BE TOWED took up most of our afternoon, so we had to wait until after school the next day to follow the caltrop lead to the castle. We were supposed to pick up the car first, but the tire shop called to tell us they only had one of the type of tire we needed so the car couldn't be fixed until Thursday. That meant we had to call a cab, which made us even madder at our saboteur, whoever they were.

One thing was clear when we finally arrived: Castle McGalliard had seen better days.

The cab dropped us off at the foot of the drawbridge in front of the dilapidated estate's hillside perch and quickly retreated down the hill toward town. We'd asked the driver to wait, but Old Man McG's reputation preceded him, and the driver was determined not to get his car—or body—filled with buckshot.

I kept a tight grip on the bag we'd picked up at the drugstore along the way. Hopefully our plan would work, because we didn't have a backup.

The castle's cracked and weathered assortment of turrets, arches, and towers loomed over us, and the whole hill loomed over Bayport's shipping docks, which were a couple of miles south of Bayport's more picturesque Inner Harbor. That stretch of the coastline was shaped like an S, with the Inner Harbor and all its quaint tourist attractions nestled inside the curve at the top. We were in the shadier, industrial part on the round peninsula down at the bottom. Filmore Johnson's cover illustration for *S&S #1* didn't have all the container ships, smokestacks, and cranes, of course, but there was no mistaking the bayside castle on the hill from the one in the comic.

There was an iron gate framed by two crumbling pillars at the mouth of the drawbridge, and each one had a date etched in the stone. One said 1432, the other 1745.

"From what Rob says, the castle was built in 1745 by the first McGalliard to come to America back before the Revolutionary War, when the colonies were still under British rule," I informed Joe.

"That's the Paul Magnus guy from the ledger Murph found, yeah?" Joe asked.

"If Murph's theory about the ledger is right," I said. "But apparently this is an exact replica of their family's ancestral castle that was built in Scotland in 1432. The American castle was empty for a while before Rob's uncle Angus emigrated from Scotland to claim it, but it's been passed down from generation to generation since it was built."

"I guess that makes Robert the next heir," Joe noted.

"In all its grandeur and the wealth of historic treasures that lie within," I said in my most pompous tone, repeating the boast I'd heard Robert make so many times at the comic shop.

"It wouldn't be hard for Sir Rob to grab a handful of antique caltrops off the shelf on his way out of the house and slip them under our tires," Joe speculated.

"We know he wanted us off the case," I replied.

"Maybe he heard we were still asking around about it at school? He does have a lot of connections at Bayport High."

Our last conversation with Robert had been more than a little suspicious, but would he really stoop to sabotage? And why? Hopefully, we'd find the answers on the other side of the castle's moat.

Joe gave the gate a shove, and it swung open easily enough.

"Lower the drawbridge!" he called across the moat.

"Um, it's already lowered," I pointed out.

Joe shrugged. "I just always wanted to say that."

The moat surrounding the castle had long ago gone dry,

and thankfully the drawbridge was in fact already down—and from the looks of the rusty gears on the other side, it had stayed that way for a long time. Looking up, I could see one of the towers on the castle's right rising higher than the rest, its battered peak standing in relief against the ominous gray sky as crows circled. A small chill went through me. Not only did it look like it had leaped straight off the pages of *Sabers & Serpents*, it looked downright frightening.

Joe walked confidently toward the castle's enormous wooden door, and I followed a little more tentatively, wondering if the cabdriver hadn't had the right idea after all.

Joe hefted the huge iron knocker and banged it against the door three times. The sound echoed around us as we waited. And waited. There was one of those little portals that slide open so the person inside can see who's there, but it remained tightly shut.

"Anybody home?! We're friends of Robert!" Joe shouted, then mumbled under his breath, "Sorta."

"If the stories about Angus never leaving the castle in the last forty years are true, then I'm guessing he's here and just not answering," I said, peering doubtfully toward the right of the castle, where a path curved through a long-neglected garden and vanished around the side.

Joe had the same thought I did but was quicker to put it into action. "Good idea, bro! Let's scope out the grounds and see if we can at least get a look in a window or something."

There were windows, all right, but most of them on this

side of the castle were high enough that you'd have to scale the wall to reach them. We passed an old well with a bucket and pulley system to the right of the tall, creepy tower at the back of the garden. Beyond that, there was another door. A normal-size one.

We were a few yards away when a ghoulish howl brought us to a stop, followed by the thump of heavy paws shaking the ground at our feet.

"Um, what is—?" Joe began to ask.

Before he could finish the thought, an enormous bloodhound with a large plastic veterinary cone around its neck came charging around the side of the castle, its huge jowls and ears flopping as it ran toward us.

I dodged out of the way, but Joe never got the chance.

"Ahhhhhhh!" he screamed as the bloodhound leaped up, putting its enormous paws on his shoulders and tackling him to the ground—where it tried to lick Joe's face with its giant tongue. Luckily for Joe, the cone prevented the dog from getting too much slobber on him.

Joe laughed as he pushed the overly friendly dog off him. "Personal space, dude, personal space!"

I reached under the dog's plastic cone of shame and flipped over the tag.

"Come here, Lucky," I said, reading the name etched above a phone number I recognized as Robert's.

Lucky swung around at his name only to clunk his plastic cone into my leg, almost knocking me over in the process.

"Ironic name choice," I said, reaching inside the plastic cone to scratch the klutzy dog's big, floppy ears as Joe made his way back to his feet. There were stitches on Lucky's rear end, which the cone was undoubtedly meant to keep him from licking.

"*WOOF*," Lucky barked as he ran back toward an oversize doggie door carved out of the regular-size door on the side of the castle—only with his cone on, his noggin was too big to fit inside, so he just smashed into the frame and pushed the entire (fortunately) unlocked door open with his face instead.

"*WOOF*," he said again, trotting through what looked like a large storage pantry and disappearing into the castle beyond.

"I'd say that counts as an invitation to enter from one of the home's residents, wouldn't you, bro?" Joe asserted confidently.

I stared at the open door. It was definitely tempting, but with Old Man McG's reputation, did we really want to risk just walking in on him?

I was still contemplating my answer when Joe decided for us and stepped inside.

"I hope we don't regret this," I said, following my brother into the dusty old pantry.

"I guess Old Man McG is a big fan of potted meat and sardines," Joe observed, running his fingers along one of the shelves, which were filled with enough tins of canned meat and fish products to last decades. "I wonder if this is part of the historic treasures Robert was bragging about."

The dusty pantry led to a less dusty but equally dilapidated and impressively large kitchen that looked like someone had given a medieval kitchen a 1970s makeover. The well-worn lime-green appliances were from the twentieth century, but the antique cast-iron pots and pans hanging from the ceiling looked like they might have been there when the castle was built in the 1700s.

The kitchen led to an antechamber with a hallway off to the side. I followed Joe past the hall into a massive dining room with chandeliers dangling two stories off the floor and an assortment of shields, spears, and trophy heads mounted on the stone walls. Daylight seeped through stained-glass windows high over our heads, depicting knights in battle.

"Now that's more like it," Joe said, admiring a pair of crossed seven-foot-tall medieval lances.

"Looks authentic, too," I said, thinking about the caltrops that had taken out our back tires.

An immense wooden table that looked like it could seat forty people occupied the center of the room. It was empty except for a candelabra in the middle and a dirty plate with sardine remnants at the head.

"I'm really not sure this is a good idea, Joe," I said, eyeing the plate of partially eaten little fishes.

"It's cool, dude," he reassured me, then cupped his hands

to his mouth and called, "We're here to help Robert out! We come in peace!"

He turned back to me as he stepped out of the dining hall. "See? No problem, bro."

"For some reason, that doesn't make me feel a lot better," I muttered, following Joe into an even larger hall with super-high ceilings and a spiral staircase vanishing under an arched stone doorway to our right. The doorway was covered by a wrought-iron gate that appeared to be bolted shut from the inside.

I gave it a small tug to confirm that it was locked and peered through the iron bars. There were a handful of swords mounted on the wall as the staircase curved out of view. I could only see the closest one clearly, but I recognized the style of the strange, wavy blade from RPG weapons guides as a flamberge. I could make out the shapes of stars and moons etched into the metal. It looked like it was straight out of a medieval fantasy tale, making the place feel even more creepy. Creepy can be fun in a role-playing game, but it's a lot more unsettling when you're sneaking around a real castle without an invitation.

"I bet that staircase leads to the weird tower we saw outside," I whispered with a shudder as I followed Joe toward the other end of the hall. "I wonder why they keep the gate to it locked when the front gate and the pantry door are both open."

"This place is huge," Joe said, looking around the room. There was a larger open doorway at the other end, guarded by an empty suit of armor on either side—I gulped—at least I hoped they were empty. One of them was wearing a plaid golf cap, which made it slightly less threatening. A long, dark tunnel curved into the distance beyond the entranceway.

Joe rapped the hatless knight on the helm with his knuckles. "Should we go through here?"

There was a cold metallic click behind us.

"To your graves is where you'll be going," growled a deep, raspy Scottish accent.

When we turned around, we were staring down the gaping barrel a three-hundred-year-old blunderbuss.

SWEET TOOTH

8

JOE

FROM ALL THE STORIES AND THE ACCENT,
it wasn't hard to guess that the short old guy
pointing an ancient pirate gun at us from behind
the locked gate to the spiral staircase was Angus
McGalliard.

Old Man McG had a big, bald head like Robert, only he
was a lot more grizzled and shorter than his nephew, and he
had a perfectly round potbelly beneath an imperfectly white
undershirt and bright red suspenders. The gun looked like
a cross between a short musket and a trumpet, with a flared
muzzle. I didn't know if a gun that old would still work, and
I didn't want to find out.

Frank stood frozen stiff with his mouth hanging open,
so it looked like it was up to me to talk our way out of this

predicament. And to be fair, I was the one who'd gotten us into it.

"Don't shoot, sir!" I pleaded. "We're friends of Robert's!"

"Ah, even more reason I should shoot ya!" he snapped.

That's when I remembered the shopping bag Frank was holding. I grabbed it out of his hand as Angus unlocked the gate and stalked toward us with his ancient gun.

"We come bearing gifts!" I shouted, holding the drugstore shopping bag out in front of me like a shield. "Tasty gifts!"

Angus snatched the bag with one hand, keeping a firm grip on the firearm with the other. I was looking for a chance to knock the gun away, but the old guy cleverly looped the bag's handles over the gun's muzzle so he could look inside with his left hand and keep his finger on the trigger with his right.

He squinted curiously into the bag and pulled out a package of assorted milk chocolates in the shapes of ghosts, bats, and jack-o'-lanterns. Robert had mentioned that his uncle could be bribed with chocolate, and I sure hoped he was right, because we didn't have a plan B.

He sneered at the bag of milk chocolates and tossed it over his shoulder.

"I prefer dark," he growled.

"I told you we should have gotten the fancy kind," Frank squeaked under his breath as Angus continued to rifle through the shopping bag full of Halloween candy.

"Ooh, peppermint patties!" he chirped with the enthusiasm of a small child.

Frank sighed deeply, his shoulders collapsing with relief. Mine kinda did too.

"You see, we come in peace," I told Angus. "And peppermint."

He stabbed his weapon's muzzle in my direction.

"What is it ye want?" has asked brusquely, keeping the gun aimed at me as he backed up toward the wall, grabbed a tattered antique chair that had probably once been pretty snazzy, and sat down so he could open the bag of peppermint patties and still threaten to shoot us at the same time. He grunted, his knee joints cracking as he eased himself into the chair.

"*Friends* of Robert," he added as he tore open the bag, emphasizing the word "friends" in about the least friendly way possible.

"I'm not sure if you heard, sir, but we're looking into the copy of *Sabers and Serpents #1* that was stolen," Frank said as politely as he could, and Frank can be pretty polite when he tries.

"You're darn right I heard it was stolen!" he barked through a mouthful of minty chocolate. "Stolen from me, by my own backstabbing nephew!"

"Wait a second, you're saying Robert stole the comic from you first?" I asked.

"He told us he found it buried in boxes of old newspapers he inherited when he moved into the castle," Frank said.

"Inherited! Ha!" Angus laughed bitterly. "I ain't croaked

yet, and till I do, Castle McGalliard and everything in it is still mine. I don't know where he dug the old rag up, but it weren't his to take."

"Do you have another copy?" asked Frank eagerly. I was pretty sure he wanted to know more as a gamer than a detective.

"Humph. Didn't know I had that one till I heard Rob got it taken from that silly shop of his. Woulda sold it meself if'n I did." He sighed and looked around at the chipped castle walls.

"No offense, Mr. McG, but Robert makes it sound like your family is worth a fortune," I told him. "Surely you don't need the money."

"Ha! Misfortune is more like it," he said.

"But Rob said you called him here from Scotland to claim his inheritance and take over as steward of your family's ancestral estate," Frank insisted.

"Aye, it's true, I called him here to be the new steward," Angus admitted. "Can't take care of this blasted place myself at my age, and somebody's got to pay the electric bill."

"I kinda figured Robert was stretching the truth when he said the castle was full of priceless treasures, but even artifacts like those suits of armor and your blunderbuss could be worth a ton to collectors if they're authentic," Frank pointed out. "If you really needed the money, I mean."

"Oh, they're priceless, all right," he said grimly. "If by priceless you mean we ain't allowed to sell them."

"Um, who's stopping you?" I asked, getting more confused by the second. "It's your castle."

"Me blighted dead ancestor, that's who!" Angus barked. "Old Paulie Magnus McGalliard, who built this place, wanted to make sure his legacy lasted forever. So the evil bugger done put it in the ancient family trust that it would be passed down from McGalliard to McGalliard until the end of time and ain't no one could ever sell it or any of what's in it. See, castle steward ain't the same as castle lord. We don't own any of it. We're just glorified caretakers."

Frank and I both gawked at him. It was like being stuck permanently footing the bill on an impractical—not to mention falling-apart—fifty-thousand-square-foot house.

"So the estate is basically worthless?" I blurted.

"And Robert still moved here all the way from Scotland to claim it?" Frank asked in disbelief.

"Hmm, might have forgotten to mention that part of the arrangement till after he got here," Angus said while casually munching on another peppermint patty.

9

BURNED

FRANK

YOU CONNED ROBERT INTO MOVING across an ocean to inherit a fortune that doesn't really exist?" Joe blurted.

I cringed at my brother's poor diplomacy skills as Angus's grip on the blunderbuss tightened. Not that I didn't share Joe's shock at the audacity of the bill of goods Angus had sold his nephew. Robert's knack for spinning tall tales apparently ran in the family, and the one that Angus used to lure his nephew to America was a doozy. No wonder Robert felt entitled to keep the comic for himself, and it wasn't part of the ancient estate either, which meant it could legally be sold if he wanted, unlike the rest of the stuff in the castle. But as outrageous as Angus's admission was, I had to question Joe's judgment antagonizing a notorious misanthrope who also happens to be pointing a gun at us.

"That's one way to put it," Angus said indignantly.

"What's the other?" Joe asked.

"I gently persuaded me only living relative to come to the aid of his helpless, lonely old uncle Angus in his hour of need," he said in a surprisingly meek voice.

"Um, no offense, sir, but I definitely wouldn't call you helpless," I said, eyeing the muzzle of his blunderbuss.

"What difference does it make? Not like he's any worse off for it," Angus snapped defensively. "My deadbeat of a nephew was broke there, an' now he's broke here. Owed money all over Scotland, he did. Had everyone from the law to the leg breakers after him to collect on debts. He should be singing me praises for getting him out of there in one piece."

Joe and I shared a glance. It explained a lot if it was true—and that was a big "if," based on how flexibly the McGalliards seemed to treat the truth. It certainly did explain Robert's nervousness around police, though. The revelation that he was hurting for money also meant something even bigger. Don Inkpen might be right: Robert had a motive to turn his copy of *Sabers & Serpents #1* into quick cash. And to threaten us off the case if he had.

Stealing from himself definitely still seemed like an extreme measure. On the other hand, setting himself up to look like a dupe by announcing an appraisal in front of the world right before it went missing would be an unexpectedly devious way to deflect suspicion.

Angus tossed the empty peppermint patty bag away in disdain and started rummaging angrily through the shopping bag for more candy that pleased him. There wasn't any dark chocolate, and I figured this was a good time to change the topic before the blunderbuss-toting curmudgeon found another reason to be unreasonably grumpy.

"I meant to mention this earlier, sir, but I'm a huge fan of the Sabers and Serpents game," I said sincerely.

He eyed me suspiciously. "You've played me game?"

"A bunch! We've been playing every week since Comic Kingdom opened. The game design is brilliant. It's as much fun to play as any fantasy role-playing game I've seen! Did you really base it all on things you found here in the castle?"

"Aye, this old albatross of a manor used to be good for something," he confirmed nostalgically. "It hadn't been lived in for generations when I arrived. Old Paulie Magnus hadn't counted on the family's fortunes fading the way they did over the years. Upkeep got too costly once hard times hit, so the McGalliard clan upped an' left Bayport, leaving the castle for Old Paulie's ghost to steward on his own. None of me American cousins wanted the headache once the inheritance reached our generation, so I claimed it. I'd been enchanted by tales of castles and quests ever since I was a wee lad and wanted to go on a quest of me own. Suppose it was that same misguided sense of adventure that led me to create Sabers and Serpents."

"I was wondering about some of the Gaelic words you used in the game and the comic, too. Those kinds of details really bring the whole S and S world to life!" I said, trying to steer the conversation toward another part of the investigation.

Angus's perpetual scowl had softened for the first time since he'd discovered the peppermint patties. He pointed the blunderbuss at Joe and nodded in my direction. "This one has taste. You shoulda let him pick the chocolate."

I saw Joe's brain preparing to crack a joke at my expense, and I elbowed him in the ribs before he could sour Angus's mood again.

"Ow," Joe grumbled.

"Did you come up with all the Gaelic words on your own?" I asked Angus, ignoring my brother. "My friends and I were trying to figure out what they mean."

"Ah, ye give me too much credit, lad. They're just pretty gibberish copied from worthless old papers I found lying around the castle. No meaning to them."

I could feel Joe starting to buzz with excitement beside me. Angus may have denied the symbols had meaning, but their origins fit with Murph's theory that the Gaelic words were code that had come from Paul Magnus McGalliard's ancient smuggler's ledger.

"Was one of the papers a map?" Joe asked eagerly.

Angus's scowl returned instantly. "That accursed map! I wish I'd never laid eyes on it!"

"Is that what's on the missing page from the other copies

of the *Sabers and Serpents* comic?" I asked, struggling to contain my own excitement.

"Argh, all it ever led to was the end of me dreams," he snarled without answering directly. "My life's work and all me savings up in flames, leaving me with nothing but a crumbling castle full of useless trinkets!"

"Um, you're talking about the warehouse fire," Joe ventured hesitantly. "And Filmore?"

"Curse that name! And the map that drove him out of his mind!" He stood up abruptly, his elderly knees creaking loudly from the effort as the chair nearly toppled over and he began pacing. "And what for? A mythical isle that doesn't even exist?"

"Filmore . . ." I hesitated and quickly backtracked as Angus swung his blunderbuss toward me. "I mean, er, your partner started the, um, all the trouble with the warehouse because of an island from the map?"

My brain was racing, trying to put the fragmented pieces Angus had told us together without accidentally saying anything that might get us shot.

"A map to nowhere on an isle that doesn't exist!" Angus erupted. "Filmore always had an irksome fondness for geography," he added bitterly. "He wasted hours studying maps of the Scottish isles after we happened on that map tucked away in an old journal, but it wasn't there to be found. The drawing was two hundred and fifty years old, and the isle mighta sunk into the sea if it had ever been there to begin with. Wasn't any more real a place than Treasure Island from me countryman Robert Louis Stevenson's famous book. 'Twas a beautifully hand-drawn map, though. Filmore and I came up with the idea to incorporate it into the story, and he drew an exact replica for the first issue. It was perfect fit for the Lost Isle we was to introduce in the comic. Had there been one!"

Angus was pacing back and forth in agitation, lost in his own thoughts. Joe opened his mouth to say something, and I put my hand on his arm, signaling him to be quiet. Angus was on a roll, and sometimes the best way to interrogate a person is to let them do their own interrogating. As much of a hermit as Angus McGalliard was, he probably didn't get many chances to even talk to people, and he'd never given so much as a single interview about what had happened with Filmore. Now that he'd started, I hoped the floodgates would stay open.

"Filmore seemed to forget about the map for a while, and if only he had!" Angus continued. "But he began acting more and more squirrelly, he did, saying he wanted to make changes to the comic, but publication was nigh and we couldn't afford to delay printing. Nay, every penny the both of us had was riding on the comic's release." Angus shook his head violently, as if trying in vain to reject the memory of it. "We was two nights from going to press when the printer called to say he'd caught Filmore breaking into his warehouse, trying to steal the printer plates and tearing the page with the map from all the proofs. The printer ran him off and changed the locks, but I was a fool and told him not to call the coppers because Filmore were my chum, or so I thought. He'd always been eccentric, he had, aye, it were part of his genius as an artist. I thought it were just jitters about the release and everything would be fine once we went to press. Only he came back to the warehouse a day later, in the dead of night, and found it locked up tight."

Angus paused and lowered his voice, a glazed look in his eyes, as if he wasn't just staring past us, but into the past itself.

"So he burned it all down instead."

"Whoa," Joe whispered in a hushed tone. "That's intense."

Angus collapsed back into the chair, exhausted from reliving the tale.

"And you never saw him again?" I asked gently.

"We'd have had some words for him if we had," he said, brandishing the blunderbuss. "Vanished like a ghost. Took the old map and all his sketches with him when he left, in case ye're wondering, as ye seem so keen on it. What is it ye want, anyway? Or did ye come to me castle just to watch a sad old man have a good chin wag?"

In a way we had—getting Angus to talk (and I figured that's what he meant about wagging his chin) was the biggest break we'd had in the case yet—but I wasn't about to tell him that. I pulled out the rusty old caltrops and cautiously walked closer so he could get a good look. "We were actually wondering if you recognized these."

"What are they, children's toys?" he asked, picking one of

the rusty, four-pronged spikes from my hand. "What's the game? If you win, you get tetanus?"

"Good one, Mr. McG," Joe chuckled.

"They're medieval antipersonnel weapons called caltrops. Someone used them to spike our tires to try to stop us from investigating the theft, and we thought they might have gotten them from your castle," I told him, gesturing to the suits of armor guarding the doorway behind us.

"Suppose it's possible there could be some lying around somewhere, but I ain't bothered to look through most of the junk here in ages," he said, handing the caltrop back to me. "Wherever they come from, you probably deserved it, nosing about in other people's business the way you do."

"Do you know who else might have had access to the castle?" I asked, ignoring the barb.

"Ask me nephew. You and he are the only ones I know been snooping around me castle."

"Well, we didn't spike our own tires, and Robert was in the comic shop when it happened," Joe retorted.

"You ain't accusing me, are ya?" Angus snarled.

"No, sir!" I insisted, eager to change the topic before Angus decided to give his blunderbuss the last word. "We're just trying to get to the bottom of who might have taken your comic, er, I mean besides Robert. You don't know anything about the person who contacted Robert to appraise the comic for Butterby's Auctioneers, do you? We think it may be connected."

"Figures that ingrate would be trying to sell something don't belong to him," Angus said in disgust. "Me own flesh 'n' blood trying to take advantage of his closest kin. Ain't nothing sacred these days?"

I bit my tongue at the irony of Angus griping about another family member trying to take advantage of him after the con he'd pulled on Robert to get him to move to Bayport.

"Well, you don't have to worry about that for now at least," Joe said. "Looks like the so-called appraiser was a scam, but we can't figure out why."

"Ain't surprised," Angus said matter-of-factly. "People been spinning yarns trying to weasel information out of me about that comic for years. Figures Robert would fall for one of them. I must be going soft in me old age too. Excepting my no-good nephew, you're the first two I've deigned to let into the castle to talk to me in near on forty years." Angus paused to think about it. "Well, other than that reporter lassie who stopped by to chat yesterday."

"Charlene was here?!" I blurted.

"Aye, she's got gumption, that one," Angus confirmed. "And better taste in chocolate than you two cheapskates."

ALL CHEWED UP

10

JOE

SHE WASN'T PLAYING AROUND AT TRYING to beat us to the scoop," I said.

"Yeah," Frank replied forlornly.

I knew he was feeling dejected that she hadn't wanted to team up to solve the case together, and from the looks of it, we could have used her help. There was something else that occurred to me about Charlene getting to Angus first. It meant she was the only other person we knew about besides Angus, us, and Robert who had access to the castle. And possibly the caltrops.

Could our school paper's most committed investigative journalist—aka my brother's current crush—want to beat us to the story so badly she'd threaten us off the case?

Charlene may not have been the warmest and fuzziest friend we had, and she clearly saw us as competition, but we'd known her for a long time, and I didn't want to think she'd do something like that. There was no way around it, though. She had a motive, and swiping the caltrops from the castle would have given her the means.

Frank was standing there looking pained, and I was debating whether to add to his dejection by sharing my theory about Charlene when an old clock chimed from somewhere inside the castle.

"Argh, you're gonna make miss my telly programs," Angus barked. "Now out with ya! I ain't got much hospitality in me, and you done used it all."

"Yes, sir!" Frank squeaked. "Thank you for talking to us!"

"If you step foot in my castle again without an invitation, it's me blunderbuss you'll be talking to," he shot back, waving the old gun threateningly.

"No, sir, Mr. McG!" I said, grabbing Frank by the arm and dragging him back toward the dining hall. "We can show ourselves out. Thanks for the chat!"

"Don't take nothing!" he shouted after us.

"Whew," Frank sighed with relief, looking over his shoulder to make sure Angus wasn't chasing after us with the blunderbuss.

Someone else was following us, though. Lucky. And he had the discarded bag of milk chocolate Halloween candies gripped in his slobbery jowls.

"Oh, no!" Frank cried. "Chocolate is toxic for dogs! It will make him sick! Come here, Lucky!"

Lucky ignored him and trotted past us. I tried to grab the bag from him, but he must have thought it was a game because he took off running into the antechamber and down the hall we'd passed on the way out of the kitchen.

"Here, boy!" I yelled, running after him with Frank close behind, as the ginormous dog looked back at us expectantly, then disappeared into an open doorway.

"Woof!" he barked as we stepped into an old study with a mixture of antique furniture, old books, and modern office equipment, including a desktop computer, a printer, and a metal filing cabinet. A portrait hanging over an old desk gave the room away as Sir Rob's home office, as it showed Robert looking absurdly pompus dressed up as an ancient Scottish royal.

The room was also where Lucky apparently kept his stash. He was crouched playfully on top of a large dog bed filled with treasure. At least it must have seemed like treasure to the oversize hound. There were a variety of well-gnawed dog toys and bones, as well as assorted chewed-up household items, including a wooden spoon, a boot, what looked like a table leg, and a mess of shredded newspapers.

"Woof!" Lucky barked again, then bent down to get the bag of chocolate. Luckily, the hound's ridiculous plastic cone knocked into the floor instead. He whimpered, trying to finagle his face close enough to the floor to grab the deadly bag of miniature pumpkins and bats.

I grabbed a decapitated stuffed lamb off the floor. "I'll distract him while you get the candy."

A few seconds later we had the chocolate, and Lucky was happily mauling his lamby.

"Whew!" Frank sighed for a second time. "I don't know how we would have explained to Robert about sneaking into the castle behind his back and poisoning his dog. Let's get out of here before anything else goes wrong. Rob could be home any minute, and I don't think he'd be happy to find us snooping around his office."

"You're a slob, Lucky," I said to the dog as I picked up a soggy, half-chewed accordion folder full of documents that didn't look like something he should be munching on. I'd originally meant just to set it back on the desk, but then I saw the label: *SRCK: Important Docs.*

SRCK wasn't a hard code to crack. Sir Robert's Comic Kingdom. I quickly started flipping through the crinkled papers inside.

"Hold on, bro," I told Frank. "There might be a copy of the phony Butterby contract in here. Robert said it was at home."

It wasn't the Butterby contract that caught my eye, though. It was a letter, dated a couple of months ago, from the Well State Insurance Company with the subject line *Rare Collectibles Policy Determination.* The letter had tooth marks in it, and some of the ink had bled from Lucky's slobber, but it was still legible. I scanned it quickly, my eyes widening as I did.

"In your RPGs, is there such a thing as a truth check?" I asked Frank.

"There's a deception check. It's kind of the same. It's what you would use to try and hide the truth, like if you wanted to use a disguise or make up a story to talk your way past a guard. How come?"

I handed Frank the torn page. "Does this count as a critical hit or a critical fail?"

Frank took the letter and read it softly out loud.

"Dear Mr. McGalliard,

While our adjuster was able to confirm the authenticity of your copy of the comic book Sabers & Serpents #1, we regret to inform you that your request for our highest level Platinum Collector's Policy for rare items worth upward of $75,000 has been denied due to the poor condition of the interior pages. As a result of the extensive staining and multiple missing pages that render the comic unreadable and inferior in condition to the specimens that have sold at auction previously, we are only able to extend a policy in the amount of $10,000 at this time.

Thank you for choosing Well State for all your insurance needs. Should you have any questions, please do not hesitate to call our toll-free number."

Frank's voice trailed off as he finished, his face looking like he'd just been sucker punched.

"It's incomplete just like the others," he spat. "Now we'll never get to see what's on that map."

He dropped the partially chewed-up document on the desk in disgust. Apparently, Sir Robert's "pristine" prized comic wasn't in any better condition than the letter once you flipped the cover.

THE TRUTH AND NOTHING BUT

11

FRANK

AN IMPRESSIVE EXTERIOR WITH A MESS of dirt and missing information hiding under the surface. Turns out the condition of Robert's copy of *S&S #1* was about as deceptive as its owner.

The discovery that pages were missing from the stolen comic hit me hard. I know it's usually best to stay emotionally detached when investigating a case, but I was more than just a detective on this one; I was also a huge RPG and comic book fan. I'd gotten almost as excited as Murph about discovering what was on the missing page, especially after Angus confirmed it was a copy of an ancient map he'd found in the castle. Sure, Angus had also said the Gaelic words were gibberish, but we'd already established that the

Bayport McGalliards weren't the most trustworthy sources of accurate information. And even if the original map really was of a place that didn't exist, it was still part of a historical mystery with ripple effects spanning three centuries! It could provide insight into transatlantic Colonial trade, it might hold the key to why Filmore sabotaged his own business, and it filled in one of the biggest blanks in comic and gaming lore.

So, yeah, as a fantasy RPG player *and* a comic book fan *and* a history buff *and* a detective (which also made me a mystery buff), this investigation had me excited on all kinds of levels. And Robert's lie about the comic containing the missing page turned a potentially hot historical case ice-cold again.

I wasn't about to let him squirm off the hook this time.

We called the cab back and headed straight from the castle to Comic Kingdom. Xephyr was behind the counter when we stalked in.

"Hail fellow adventurers!" she greeted us cheerily, looking up from the miniature fantasy figures she was painting. "How goeseth the detecting? Have you cracked the case?"

"Working on it," Joe said noncommittally.

"If I don't crack Robert first," I mumbled under my breath.

"Not going so good, huh?" She frowned when she noticed my expression. "Any exciting leads at least?"

"We were hoping to talk to Robert about that, actually," I

said, thinking that it was curious Robert hadn't told Xephyr he'd technically fired us after we found out the auction appraisal was a scam.

"Sorry, guys, it's just me holding the fort until he comes back to close at nine. He's running the show all day tomorrow, though. Want me to give him a message for you when he comes in?" she asked.

"That's okay, Xeph, we can just try to catch him later," I replied.

Robert's cell phone was going straight to voice mail, and Joe and I both had tests at school the next day, so hanging out until nine waiting for him wasn't an option. Studying for my math test probably wasn't going to help us find Robert's comic or discover what was on that map, but things I'd learned in class had cracked cases for us before, so it might still come in handy on another mystery someday. As for our current mystery, we'd have to come back the next afternoon after school let out.

"Definitely doesn't look like the theft has hurt business any," Joe commented, looking around the small shop that was still busy close to dinnertime. People were milling around, flipping through comics. A bunch of kids were at the gaming tables, and from the looks of it, they were all playing Sabers & Serpents.

"It's wild how much publicity it has gotten," Xephyr said. "It's all over social media, and Robert's been working the podcast circuit, giving interviews and hyping it up in online forums. It's really driving interest in the Sabers and Serpents revival and the store, too. We've been busier than ever the past couple days, and the web server can barely keep up with the traffic the website's been getting from all the people trying to download the S and S rules and character sheets since the original manuals are out of print."

I scowled. Another way Robert was benefitting from the theft. I wondered if he had the rights to post his uncle's game online or if he'd taken that without asking too.

I looked up at the no-longer-empty space over the counter where the stolen glass case containing *Sabers & Serpents #1* had been. In its place was a large, glossy poster.

By Invitation Of
Sir Robert's Comic Kingdom

Hear ye! Hear ye! Come one, come all,
to the most spooktacular party of the century!
Sir Robert's Royal Halloween Masquerade Ball
This Friday, October 31 • Castle McGalliard
Where the Sabers & Serpents legend was born
and heads are sure to roll,
chilling secrets will be revealed!
COSTUMES REQUIRED
Live entertainment, light refreshments,
and unimaginable fear provided.
See you there—if you dare!

"So he really is going through with the party even without the comic to reveal," I observed, wondering what kind of "chilling secrets" he had in mind.

"Doesn't it look awesome?!" Xephyr gushed over the poster.

"You know, it really does," Joe conceded, and I had to agree. As annoyed as I was with the host, it was hard not to be excited about a huge Halloween costume party at a real castle.

"He's still going to do the webcast at midnight too," Xephyr informed us. "He's been telling everyone he's going to reveal a major hint about what was on the missing page. It's not as cool as being able to show the real comic, I guess, but everybody is still super stoked about it. It's kind of even more mysterious, you know?"

"Yeah," I said, not telling her it was a mystery her boastful boss didn't actually have a clue how to solve.

My math test on Thursday was thankfully fairly easy, because the case had kept my brain tied in knots all that night and the next day at school. Joe and I were both stumped trying to figure out what else Comic Kingdom's head of state had up his sleeve.

To make matters worse, Charlene gave me the cold shoulder when I tried to ask her at lunch if she wanted to trade information. Joe had shared his suspicions with me about her being our saboteur, and maybe even worse. Not that it hadn't occurred to me, too, but I was kind of in denial about it. I really liked Charlene and wanted to give her the benefit of the doubt. I knew how seriously she took the profession of journalism. We'd even had conversations about how investigative journalism's ability to expose corruption and reveal the truth was one of the very foundations of a healthy democracy. I also knew how competitive she was, and I wasn't sure she wouldn't resort to dirty tactics to be the first to break a story.

I decided not to think about her motives and turned back to the mystery itself. I went over what we'd learned.

Angus had told us that Sir Robert had been totally broke and in debt back in Scotland. The file Lucky led us to showed that Robert had lied about the condition—and value—of his copy of *S&S #1*.

We'd originally suspected that Robert staged the theft of the comic to try to collect the insurance money and then sabotaged our car to warn us off the case. But the comic was only worth $10,000, which was a lot less than Sir Robert had led everyone to believe. Ten thousand dollars was still a lot of money, but it wasn't the type of windfall that could make you rich, and committing a major crime like insurance fraud seemed like a huge risk to take. Not to mention the fact that he didn't want the police involved, and you can't make an insurance claim without a valid police report. So that theory was out the window.

Then there was the fake Butterby's appraiser, and we

couldn't make heads or tails of how Robert could profit from a fake auction. Plus, he had seemed genuinely surprised when we told him the appraiser who contacted him was an imposter.

Finally, there was the theft of the comic book. Sir Robert had seemed devastated by that, too. He even pleaded with us to investigate right after the robbery. Why would he do that if he had stolen the comic himself?

Robert had proven himself a pretty good actor, and I didn't put it past him to fake being upset to sell the crime. But as tall and over-the-top as his tales could be, they seemed calculated to achieve an effect. Robert was logical, and there didn't seem to be anything logical about any of this.

One thing was for sure, though. We weren't going to figure it out without more information. We were short on facts, and it looked like there was only one way we were going to get them. Not that pinning Robert down on the real story would be easy.

Robert could make up all the bogus stories he wanted and claim they were true, but that didn't change the fact that *facts are facts* and you can't ignore them or make up "alternatives," no matter how much they might incriminate you or make you look bad. We had our work cut out trying to parse fact from fiction when it came to Sir Rob. But it didn't matter if you were the make-believe ruler of a "Comic Kingdom" or president of the United States—there was only one truth, and no one was powerful enough to change it. As detectives, it was our job to find it and make sure justice was done.

We were back at Comic Kingdom to take it up with the man himself as soon as school let out. The shop was hopping, and Sir Robert was holding court at the counter, regaling a rapt crowd of elementary school kids with tall tales. He was so engrossed in his own story, he didn't even bother to look up when the door chimed, so we hung back and listened in, and I nearly broke my eye sockets from eye-roll strain.

"The thief was dressed from head to toe in black like a ninja, and he might well have been one, for I've never seen a man move with such stealth and agility, not even on my undercover spy fighting missions for Her Majesty's Secret Service. But I was undeterred. I chased the dastardly comic swindler through the darkened alley, armed with nothing but my wits and a burning desire for justice. I dodged out of the way of every dart and dagger he threw at me and was nearly upon him when—*POOF!* He vanished like a ghost into the fog. Had I been wearing better arch supports, you can bet I would have had him!"

The kids oohed and aahed. I shook my head.

"Wow, sounds like you've been busy since we last saw you, Rob," Joe quipped as we stepped up to the counter.

Robert's face sagged with apprehension when he saw us, but he quickly replaced the look with a gleaming smile.

"Ah, if it isn't the Hardy lads! No hard feelings about the

other day, yeah? Sometimes you just have to take matters into your own hands. I'm sure you understand." He turned back to the elementary school kids. "These young men are fine detectives, fine. If you ever need a master crime solver and ol' Rob isn't around, you give them a call." He winked at his young audience.

"Thanks for the reference, Rob," Joe deadpanned.

"Don't mention it. Always happy to help a friend," he replied merrily.

"We heard you're still planning a big reveal at the party to tell everyone more about that missing page," I said casually.

"That crook may have robbed me of my comic, but they can't rob me of my memory." He tapped his bald head. "Every detail of that page is etched in my brain with precision. I made a promise to the comic book world, and Sir Rob is always good for his word!"

"I'm sure the insurance company will be happy to hear it when they write you that record-breaking ten-thousand-dollar check," I said, sliding Lucky's former chew toy from my jacket and dropping it on the counter in front of him.

A momentary look of confusion gave way to one of full panic when he saw the Well State Insurance Company letterhead atop the slightly mauled letter. He quickly snatched it off the counter and clutched it to his chest, hiding the real revelation about the comic's still-missing page from the prying eyes of the elementary school kids.

"I guess your uncle Angus didn't mention our visit to the

castle," Joe said. "We took this away from Lucky on the way out. Didn't think you'd want papers as important as this to get, ahem, damaged."

Robert glanced at the door like he might make a run for it, but looked around the crowded shop and thought better of it.

"Perhaps we can chat later," he pleaded. "After business hours? Lots of loyal customers depending on ol' Rob, and we wouldn't want to inconvenience them."

"Perhaps not," Joe replied.

"We can have this discussion in front of your friends here and the rest of your customers, or you can kick everyone out again if you want, but we've got questions and we're not leaving until we get some answers," I said bluntly.

Robert sighed and hit a button on the register, popping open the cash drawer. He reached inside, and for a second I thought he was going to try and bribe us, but he pulled out a five-dollar bill and slapped it on the counter in front of a small, curly-haired kid with thick glasses.

"Percy, you're in charge while I step outside for a top secret Halloween party conference with the Hardys."

"But I don't know how to work the register," Percy objected, still eyeing the bill hopefully.

"I have faith in you, lad," Robert replied, reaching over the counter, physically lifting Percy up, and setting him on the stool on the other side. "Anybody wants to buy anything, tell them I'll be right back. Anybody steals anything while I'm gone and I'll hang you from the rack in the castle's dungeon."

Robert marched confidently through his kingdom, past Dennis and a bunch of other kids at the game tables, through the back room, and out the rear door of the shop, with us right behind. The second we were in the alley and out of sight, he dropped down to his knees and started begging.

"Please, have mercy on me—you can't tell anybody," he pleaded.

"Tell us the real deal with the comic and we'll think about it," Joe said.

"And the auction scam," I added.

"And being broke," Joe included.

"Basically, stop lying and start talking straight," I said.

"Or we're going straight to the cops," Joe said.

"And the press," I said. "I know someone who's itching to print the real scoop."

"If she hasn't gotten it already," Joe said. "We weren't the only ones to pay a visit to Uncle Angus."

Joe and I tag-teamed him with the bad-cop/bad-cop routine, and he shrank with every blow.

"You two are worse than back-alley leg breakers back home," he said.

"All we want is the truth," I said.

"Now spill," Joe concluded.

Robert sighed deeply and sat down on a stack of wooden crates. "Figures Lucky would be the one to out me. A mate got him for me from a rescue shelter for police dogs, ironically. Poor Lucky didn't make the cut. Apparently, the undisciplined beast had a tip-top nose but wasn't very good at following protocol."

"I don't know about your nose, but the not-following-protocol part sounds like a good match. You were supposed to be telling us the truth about the comic," Joe reminded him.

"You've got the letter, so you know the page is missing," he said. "I nearly collapsed from excitement when I first found it buried amid the junk in the castle. And then I opened the cover. Flipped past the first few pages and an entire fistful of pages were torn right out, and what was left was soaked through with ink stains and brown blotches. It's a miracle the cover looked as good as it did, and lucky that. Least it was at the time. Figured as long as I kept it under glass, no one would be the wiser."

"And you could trick everyone into thinking it was the world's only complete copy and Sir Rob was the only person on earth who knew the secret of what was inside," I stated accusingly.

"A good myth is worth more in free marketing than the money the insurance company said it was worth. Not that I couldn't have used the money. I sank the last of my savings into the shop after I moved. A boyhood dream to own a comic shop, you know? Sure, ten grand could have helped pay the bills in the short term, but I figured having that bad boy behind the counter gave me the fighting edge I needed to make a go of it. And it did at that. Until that blasted con artist Leadbetter—or whoever he really was—called."

Joe chuckled.

"You find my misery funny, do you?" Robert asked, looking genuinely hurt.

"Sorry, dude, just found it a little comical you calling someone else a con artist," Joe explained.

"Point taken," Robert conceded with a sigh. "I suppose I wasn't *entirely* honest with everyone."

I cleared my throat conspicuously.

"Fine, I've more hot air in me than the Hindenburg, but that doesn't make me a bad person. I've got hopes and dreams too. And a little white lie about the comic didn't hurt anyone. I'd say the mystery of it even gave folks a bit of joy. And I doubt anyone would be playing Sabers and Serpents again after all these years if I hadn't made a to-do of it."

"I'll give you that," I said. The missing page may have been a myth, but Robert's salesmanship of that mythology had managed to breathe new life into a classic RPG that had given me hours of entertainment. "But what were you going to do when you actually had to show the comic to Leadbetter if he had been a real auction appraiser? Everyone would have known you were a liar as soon as you opened the cover on that webcast."

"Or was the phony Butterby appraisal just another part of your scam?" Joe asked.

"It wasn't a scam!" he insisted, but then he paused to think about it for a second. "Okay, it was a scam, but not the way you think! I thought the call from Butterby's was real! It was them I was trying to scam, only the blasted scammer scammed me first!"

"Come again?" I said, my head spinning with trying to figure out all the permutations of who was scamming whom.

"I'd planned to keep that comic under glass forever until Wendell Leadbetter called and guaranteed me a hundred large sight unseen if I'd give them exclusive rights to sell my copy of S and S at auction," he said, shoulders slumping.

"A hundred thousand dollars?!" Joe and I both blurted at the same time. Joe added a whistle for good measure.

"That's what I said," Robert said wistfully. "Leadbetter told me he thought they could get $125,000 at least for a complete copy based on how much the last one with a missing page went for. He'd heard I'd refused to sell and wanted to make it worth my while. Said he knew he couldn't guarantee what a buyer might pay at auction, so the auction house would take the risk and make the guarantee instead. All I had to do was sign the contract and hand both it and the comic over at the party. Whether it sold for one dollar or a million, they'd pay me a minimum of a hundred K as soon as it sold. The only guarantee I had to make was that it was authentic."

"So I'm guessing you definitely didn't stage the theft so you could collect the insurance money, then," Joe surmised.

"Certainly not! I would have been throwing away my

own golden goose. That comic was worth ten times more to me than to whoever stole it!" he protested.

I gave Robert a hard look and he didn't flinch. I believed him.

"So you signed the contract?" I asked.

"Of course I signed! I was going to make a killing on a comic I knew was worth only a fraction of what they were offering me. It was worth a lot of marketing dollars behind glass, but not that many."

"What were you going to do when you actually had to open it up at the party? Everyone in the world would know you were blowing smoke," said Joe.

"I'd have a hundred-thousand-dollar last laugh! I fancy my reputation, but I fancy a whole heaping grip of green-backs a lot more. Aye, it might even have boosted my reputation in certain circles. A hustle like that would have been legendary. And it was entirely legal. Unlike some of my hustles back in Scotland, if I'm entirely honest."

I raised a skeptical eyebrow. Was Robert McGalliard *ever* entirely honest?

"Only we found out Leadbetter was too good to be true and the joke was on you," Joe reminded him.

"Yeah, that," he agreed sadly.

"Which is why you were even more distraught when we told you about Leadbetter than you were when the comic was stolen," I said. "Even if we got it back, you knew you couldn't get more than ten thousand for it."

"So what was in it for the phony Leadbetter?" Joe wondered. "Is the auction scam somehow linked to the theft? Or was he angling to steal the comic from you on Halloween and someone beat him to the punch?"

"If the phony Leadbetter was planning to steal the comic and then got wind of the theft, that would certainly explain why he ghosted," I said.

"You're the detectives," Robert replied. "All I know is I want to punch whoever's behind it, not that it would do me much good. That comic's only worth ten thousand dollars to me whether I have it or not."

"No wonder you tried to call us off the investigation after we discovered the appraiser was a fake!" I exclaimed, the pieces of Robert's opportunistic puzzle starting to click together. "You didn't want the comic found! If it stays stolen, you can at least collect the insurance money *and* still pretend you know what's on the missing page to make yourself look good and promote the shop."

When Robert looked down at his feet, I knew I had it right.

"You couldn't sell it for more if we found it anyway, and as long as it didn't turn up, no one would have to know you lied," I concluded.

"Or at least they wouldn't have if we hadn't figured out you were pulling a fast one," Joe pointed out.

"You can't tell! Please! I've cooperated! I told you everything I know!" Robert implored us desperately. "The bad publicity could kill my business, and I need Comic Kingdom. And my loyal subjects need me. That shop is my life."

"You should have thought about that before you tangled your own web with all the lies you've been weaving," Joe replied.

"Frank, please! Have mercy on a poor sinner," he begged, turning away from Joe and grabbing hold of my arm with both hands. "Not just for me, but for my aged, meek, decrepit, helpless, sad, sad, sad old uncle Angus. He's depending on me to pay the bills. He'll freeze during the winter without the income from the shop to keep the fires burning. You have no idea how expensive it is to heat a house the size of a, well, castle."

"Don't forget, we've met your uncle. 'Meek' and 'helpless' definitely isn't the way I'd describe him," I said. "But . . ."

I looked at Joe and could tell we were on the same page.

"His lies were pretty scuzzy, but not exactly illegal," Joe admitted, then turned back to Robert. "Unless you lied to the police, but we can leave that to your new buddy Chief Olaf to untangle for himself."

"There is also the question of whether the comic really belongs to you or your uncle, since he says you took it without his permission," I said as Robert continued to plead with his eyes. "But given what Angus also told us about how he tricked you into coming to America to pay his bills for him, we'll leave that between the two of you to figure out as well."

"You know, it may also work to our advantage to keep

the thief and the phony auction appraiser in the dark that we know the comic's real condition," Joe reflected. "The thief has got to know, but the fake Leadbetter may not, and we may be able to catch someone else in a lie about it as well."

I fixed Robert with another hard stare. "We're not going to stop investigating, though, so I can't promise you the truth won't eventually come out when we find the thief. But we will consider keeping it a secret for now on two conditions."

He looked at me expectantly. "Anything."

"First, stop lying," I said. "That means no more telling people you know what's on that missing page. You don't have to confess the whole thing, but if anybody else wants you to talk about *Sabers and Serpents #1*, just say it's part of an ongoing investigation and you can't discuss it. And that includes at the party."

"Meaning no live webcast with made-up chilling secrets about what's inside the comic, either," Joe added.

"I . . . I'll try," he said with pained resignation. "What's the second condition?"

Joe turned to look at me. "Yeah, I was kind of wondering that myself."

I grinned. "Robert agrees to lend me Lucky for my Halloween costume."

SWORD IN THE FOAM

FOAM

12

JOE

HAT DO YOU MEAN YOU WON'T TELL me what your costume is?" I protested.

"It's a chilling secret," said Frank, still grinning.

"But I'm your own brother!"

"I want it to be a surprise," Frank said resolutely.

"Fine, then I won't tell you what I'm going as either," I huffed.

"Funny, I don't think I asked," said Frank annoyingly. I love my brother, but he can also be one of the most infuriating people I know.

"Whatever. It doesn't matter anyway. We live in the same house and share a bathroom," I said. "We're going to see each other's costumes before anyone else anyway."

Frank shrugged. "Still not gonna tell you before we get ready."

"As intriguing as the mystery of Frank's costume is, do you think it's all right if I get back to my shop now?" Robert said. "I can't say I'm totally confident that young Percy was up to the managerial task with which I entrusted him, and I do still have a business to run." He paused and bowed toward us. "Thanks to you kind and generous souls, of course. Now if you boys don't mind . . ." He gestured to the door.

"Lead the way," I said, opening the back door and scowling at my brother and that smug secret-keeping grin of his.

"How did you convince Angus to let you have a Halloween party at the castle anyway?" Frank asked as we walked inside. "Your uncle struck me as a lot of things, but a gracious host wasn't one of them."

"Aye, it was easy," Robert replied, stepping from the back room into the shop. "I threatened to stop paying the electric bill and head home to Scotland."

I shook my head in amusement. "You two sure do make for interesting roommates."

"He did threaten that anyone who goes near his tower will get shot in the bum, though, so I'll be advising my guests to steer clear lest they want to leave the castle with a trouser-load of buckshot as a party favor," Robert said, not seeming all that concerned.

"Seems like a sound plan," I said, with my tongue firmly

planted in my cheek. I couldn't imagine what could possibly go wrong with a misanthropic, trigger-happy, blunderbuss-toting hermit playing cohost to a party full of people.

"The old recluse usually doesn't roam much beyond his tower or the kitchen, so I figure I'll just rope that wing off," he said. "I'll have enough fake blood to clean up, don't want to add any of the real stuff to the chore list."

His mouth dropped open as we approached the counter, where Percy was counting through a neatly stacked pile of cash and jotting notes on a notepad.

"Hey, boss," he said casually. "I couldn't open the register to make change, so I rounded everything up except for the credit card purchases. For those, I wrote the numbers, expiration dates, and three-digit codes down for you to run later. I hand-wrote receipts in duplicate so both you and the customer would have transaction records. Nobody tried any funny business, except one guy in a Slytherin T-shirt tried to pocket a Dalek key chain, but Max caught him and tossed him out."

Percy nodded at a girl with red hair, who looked about twelve, standing guard next to the counter. She nodded back and cracked her knuckles.

"Well, I'll be. We'll have to let Xephyr know she's got some competition for her job," Robert said.

"We figure a ten percent commission for me running the bank and five for Max working security should cover our trouble," Percy said.

"But I already gave you five dollars!" Robert complained.

"That was my signing bonus," Percy replied. "And you still owe Max hers."

"And I thought the Hardys drove a tough shakedown," Robert sighed, opening the register and counting out the cash. "The four of you could team up and give them Edinburgh loan-shark operations a run for their money."

Percy and Max exchanged a high five, pocketed their payout, and headed for the front door. Which reminded me of the shiny new lock I'd seen on the back door when we reentered the shop from the alley.

"Did Chief Olaf's investigation turn up any forensic evidence on the broken back-door lock or the wall where the glass case was?" I asked Robert.

"Not much, unfortunately," he replied. "They dusted for prints, but there weren't any behind the counter or in the back that shouldn't have already been there."

I nodded. Picking up useful prints in a business with a lot of foot traffic is a long shot.

Robert continued, "A security camera in the restaurant on the corner caught footage of a person dressed in all black wheeling a suitcase the size of the display case out of the alley at 12:04 a.m. on Sunday, but it was too dark to pick up any identifying features."

"A person dressed in black, huh? I guess we know where the whopper you told those kids about you chasing a ninja came from," I said.

Robert shrugged, a little smile pulling at his lips. "What? It could have happened."

I chuckled. He had a vivid imagination, I had to give him that.

"Well, at least now we have a time stamp on the crime," Frank said. "Assuming the ninja's our perp and wasn't just out for a midnight stroll with their luggage, that would put the theft at shortly before midnight, depending on how long it took them to break the lock on the door."

"Apparently not long," Robert begrudgingly admitted. "The police said the lock wasn't very good to begin with, and the threading on the screws was already partially stripped. All they think it took was a hammer and a chisel."

I was going to remind him about that fancy security system he'd lied about hooking up but stopped myself. It isn't cool to rub a person's nose in it when they're already down. He'd already lost his prized possession and what he thought was going to be a hundred-grand payday. I didn't need to make him feel even worse.

"Speaking of broken things, how did my Halloween canine companion get that stitched-up cut on his tush?" Frank asked, shifting the conversation back to Lucky and his infuriatingly mysterious Halloween costume. "Not that I can't make good use of that collar of his on Friday."

"Your guess is as good as mine," Robert said. "That dog's always getting into something he shouldn't. It's not the first time he's had to wear one of those ridiculous collars. You can make it your next case if you want."

"I think this case is plenty for now, thanks," I said. Frank and I had more pressing things to think about than Lucky's rear end. Including the party.

Robert's Halloween bash was just about the only thing anyone wanted to talk about at school the next day. Frank had started a trend with the rest of the Bayport Adventurers Guild, and almost everybody was keeping their costumes a secret until they unveiled them at the party that night, which was the most annoying thing ever. I was dying to talk about my costume, but I wasn't about to cave when no one else would.

Frank and I had a close ear to everyone's conversations, but if anyone at school was involved in the Sabers & Serpents case, they weren't letting on. I'd planned on keeping an eye on Charlene in particular, but that turned out to be pointless as well, because she wasn't there. I checked with her editor at the newspaper, and they said she'd called in sick.

We went back by Comic Kingdom after school to see if she'd done any more snooping around the shop and to hit Robert with some follow-up questions. Sir Rob was in the middle of a transaction when we walked in, selling a customer a foam samurai sword from the rack of LARP weapons hanging next to the counter.

"Hard to believe they aren't real blades," Frank

commented as the customer left. "Every batch of weapons Xephyr makes gets even more impressive. Amazing that they're made from foam and latex and not real steel."

"They're some of our bestsellers," Robert said proudly. "I had her make me a custom Scottish claymore for my costume, which I shan't be revealing either, in case you were wondering."

"I don't want to know anyway," I grumbled, although I kinda really did.

I picked up a long sword up from the rack. Frank wasn't joking about the quality. Until you held it and felt the texture of the handle and the difference in weight, the arsenal looked like dead ringers for real medieval axes, swords, and assorted other weapons. There was even a fearsome-looking spiked ball-and-chain flail. They all had intricate designs and super-detailed paint jobs to make them look old and distressed.

"Hold on a second," Frank said, eyeing a sword with an extra-long handle and a wavy curved blade that looked a bit like a flattened slithering snake with stars and moons etched in it. "I just saw a flamberge sword like that."

"It does look familiar, doesn't it?" Robert agreed.

"Has Xephyr been to the castle?" Frank asked him.

"Nope. I'll be breaking my cranky old uncle's no-visitors rule for the first time at the party this evening," he said. "In grand scale, I might add."

"And you didn't give her a picture or anything to make this from?" Frank asked seriously.

"No. Except for my claymore, the designs are all Xephyr's own," Robert replied.

"This one isn't just hers," Frank declared. "It's an exact replica of a sword from the castle."

"Are you sure? I know I've seen it before, but I can't quite place it," Robert said.

"Probably because it's behind the locked gate blocking Angus's tower," Frank said. "If you look closely through the gate, you can see it right before the staircase curves out of sight."

"Which means Xephyr must have been in that part of the castle to see it!" I exclaimed. No wonder the sword had Frank so agitated! He had taken a closer look through the bars of Angus's gated tower entrance than I had, which was why I hadn't recognized it. Xephyr definitely shouldn't have been able to recognize it either. "Angus told us we were the only people except for Robert and Charlene he'd let into the castle to talk to him in years."

"Yup," Frank confirmed. "So either Angus is lying about his guest list, or Xephyr's been inside the castle on her own."

13

FRANK

I THINK WE KNOW WHO WE NEED TO TALK TO NEXT," Joe said.

"You think Xephyr is involved somehow?" Robert asked incredulously.

"I don't want to jump to conclusions," I said. "There could be an innocent explanation, but it does seem suspicious that she would have been inside the castle to see that sword."

"Well, we know she was away all night at the LARP campout in Bayport Heights with Dennis when the shop was robbed, so she isn't a suspect in the robbery at least," Joe interjected.

Robert looked relieved to hear it. We'd all seen the pictures of her on the camping trip in her werebear costume.

Lots of players, including Xephyr, had posted live updates until well after midnight, which was the same time the surveillance camera on the corner captured our black-clad suspect rolling the suitcase away from Comic Kingdom.

"We'll know more once we talk to her. She'll be our first priority tonight at the party," I said. "And truth is, it's not like we have a lot of other leads to go on at this point."

"I have faith in you, lads," Robert said. "And speaking of parties, I've got to close up early and head back to the castle to finish getting ready." He cupped his hands to his mouth and called out to the shop full of customers. "Last call, citizens! The Kingdom closes in fifteen minutes! I'll see you all at the castle this evening for the Halloween party to end all Halloween parties!"

Joe may have been right about us living together and sharing a bathroom, but I still managed to keep my costume a secret. He was waiting for me right outside my bedroom when I opened the door, but I kept the rest of my costume hidden under the caped houndstooth overcoat I was wearing and in the large canvas tote bag I was carrying.

"Really?!" Joe asked, shooting me the stink eye.

"Really," I said.

Joe hadn't made good on his threat to keep his costume a surprise. I think he was too excited. He was dressed like one of the Keystone Cops, the bumbling old-school policemen from the classic black-and-white slapstick movies. He had on a long blue coat and a goofy domed hat, and he was carrying a billy club, just like the characters always did. That wasn't the part of the costume that had him giddy, though. It was the Bayport PD shield on the helmet and the sheriff's star on his chest with the name CHIEF OLAF written on it.

"What do you think?" he asked, grinning.

"I think the chief might throw in you jail," I said, laughing. "But I'll definitely bail you out, because your costume is awesome. Now let's get over to the castle. I have to get Lucky in costume before we go into the party."

Castle McGalliard looked both spookier and safer than the last time we'd been there. It was definitely scary-looking at night, especially with all the plastic skeletons dangling from the gates and the jack-o'-lanterns flickering in the castle's windows. Thankfully, all the cars lining the drive leading up to the drawbridge and the happy costumed partygoers piling inside made it feel less like we were walking into an actual haunted house.

"Robert really pulled it off," Joe said admiringly. "We got here early and it looks like half the town already beat us."

I scoped out the guests around us, looking for any of the folks on our Persons of Interest list. Xephyr and Charlene both made the list. We were also going to be keeping a close eye on Robert, looking for an opportunity to have another chat with Angus (if we could find a good opening without getting shot at), and watching to see if Don Inkpen crashed his comic shop rival's party. I'd hoped to enlist Murph's help casing the crowd, but I think I'd hurt his feelings when I wouldn't share confidential details about the investigation with him earlier that day at school, and he wasn't texting me back. He could be a little sensitive like that, and one of the reasons I wanted to find him was to apologize and explain that it wasn't personal. Unlike Lucky and Robert, I did like to follow protocol, and controlling the flow of information on a case was always a smart move. My apology would have to wait, though. I didn't see Murph or anyone else on the list. They were either hidden behind masks or they weren't among the crowd making their way inside.

"I'm going around to the kitchen to rendezvous with Lucky," I said to Joe. "Keep an eye out for our people of interest and I'll meet up with you inside."

I found Lucky at the side door, waiting to slobber on me. Robert wasn't there, but there was a leash with a note taped to the doorknob.

Thanks for watching the stubborn beast for me. If he breaks anything, you pay for it.

"Figures," I said out loud to Lucky. "Now let's get you into costume!"

He barked agreeably as I removed his cone of shame and replaced it with the one I'd picked up and painted with green glow-in-the-dark paint.

"The perfect spectral hound!" I complimented him. I couldn't tell, but it looked like he was smiling. "Usually the mysterious monster doesn't help the detective crack the case, but we can make an exception this time."

I pulled out my magnifying glass along with an old-fashioned prop pipe, and put on my classic houndstooth deerstalker cap: a wool hat with tied-up ear flaps and bills in both the front and the back.

"It's elementary, my dear Lucky," I said in a bad British accent. "Let's go!"

I would say I walked Lucky around to the castle's front door, but it was more like him walking me! He practically dragged me behind him as he made a beeline for the party. I was starting to rethink the wisdom of borrowing the big bloodhound as he bowled his way through a trio of witches and snatched a candy apple out of the hand of Thor.

"Sorry!" I called to the god of thunder as I tried to rein Lucky in. He was happy to take a break and plop down now that he had something to munch on.

I paused to take in the enormous hall past the castle's front door. The rooms we'd been in before were big, but this one took the oversize cake. It really was the perfect place for a Halloween party. Robert barely even had to decorate. The crowd's costumed vampires, executioners, and knights all looked like they were already at home amid the castle's damp, medieval-artifact-adorned stone walls. There was even a live band with a flute, a lute, and a fiddle all dressed up as recently murdered medieval bards. I deduced the recently murdered part by all the fake blood and prop knives and arrows sticking out of them.

The place was already filled with Bayport residents of all ages in all kinds of costumes, and more were streaming in by the minute. It wouldn't be surprising if half the town showed up. I mean, how often do you get to go to a masquerade ball in a real castle?!

People had really stepped up their costume game for the event. I didn't know if Robert planned to give out any awards for best costume, but I already had a couple of front-runners (I mean, besides myself, of course!). It was impossible not to grin at the little kid dressed up as a vampire hot dog, replete with full-body wiener suit, bloody fangs, and a Dracula cape. And the fantasy fan in me got a kick out of a comedic wizard who looked like a cartoon version of Merlin or Gandalf. They had a mane of long white hair, a bulbous nose poking out of an absurdly huge white beard, and a peaked wizard's cap pulled all the way down over their forehead to their comically bushy fake eyebrows.

The crowd's costumes were top notch, but I still didn't see any of the people we were looking for. I recognized a couple of kids from our LARPs and the shop, including Percy and Max dressed as magician Kiel and cyborg Charm from the Story Thieves books, but there was no sign of Robert, Xephyr, or anyone else on our list. With all the elaborate costumes and masks, it was going to be hard to pick anyone out. I did see Joe, though.

"Sherlock Holmes!" he yelled as he strode over carrying a half-eaten corn dog. "I should have guessed from the coat. But what's Lucky supposed to be?"

Joe gave my canine sidekick a scratch behind the ears.

"You're a better detective than that," I chided him. "I'm Sherlock from Sir Arthur Conan Doyle's third Holmes novel, *The—*"

"*Hound of the Baskervilles*," I heard Charlene declare curtly.

I turned to see her standing behind me in a strawberry-blond wig and a well-tailored pink plaid coat with a large magnifying glass gripped in one hand and a vintage flashlight sticking out of her coat pocket. Lucky woofed and ran over to her for a jowl scratch. It was obvious they were already acquainted.

"Hey, Luck," she said a lot less curtly. "The spectral green paint for the supernatural hound is a nice touch."

In the book, Sherlock Holmes is on the case of a supposedly supernatural, murderous hound. Lucky obviously fell short on the murderous part, but I was impressed Charlene had gotten it right away.

"Clever," she added begrudgingly.

"Thanks, Charlene!" I said, impressed with myself for impressing her.

"But not clever enough to crack this case before I do," she said, the gruffness returning to her voice. Boy, she really was good at bursting my bubbles.

Her costume rang a bell, but I couldn't quite place it until I saw the HELLO MY NAME IS . . . sticker she was wearing, with the name *Nancy* written beneath it.

"Nancy Drew!" I said. Nancy was another real-life teen

detective, and her master sleuthing had made national headlines a few times. We'd actually teamed up with her to solve a big case last Christmas and became friends—well, I mean, after she got over thinking we were suspects!

"Hey, we're all dressed as investigators!" Joe said. "It's like life imitating art. Or, um, art imitating life. Or Halloween imitating life imitating art?"

While Joe was busy mixing metaphors, I grabbed the opening to try to thaw the ice with Charlene over the investigation. "Since our costumes all share a theme, maybe we can still team up to crack the case together. If we shared information, we could—"

"Nice try, Sherlock, but I almost have it cracked already, and there's no way I'm letting anyone else beat me to the scoop on this story," she said, pivoting around and marching in the other direction.

"But we both have magnifying glasses!" I protested uselessly, feeling my stomach drop as I turned to Joe. "She's pretty determined, huh?"

"The question is *how* determined?" he asked pointedly. "Sounds to me like she'd do just about anything to stop us from solving it first."

It made my stomach drop even more to admit it, but Charlene clearly had a motive to deflate our investigation, possibly along with our tires. Until we could rule her out, she was still a suspect as our caltrop saboteur.

"Think we should tail her?" Joe asked.

"No, she'll be on the lookout for it. Let's just keep an eye on her and focus on the others on our list," I said. "If she really is that close to solving the case, we'll find out soon enough. I don't want her to think we really are trying to steal the scoop from her. We can crack this on our own."

"I thought I told you to stay away from the Comic Kingdom investigation," Chief Olaf snapped from over Joe's shoulder.

"Oh, hey, Chief!" Joe said, wheeling around. "We weren't talking about *that* case. We were talking about the pretend case our Halloween alter egos are working on."

Joe pointed to our costumes and tried to give Chief Olaf his most convincing innocent grin.

The chief was wearing a fake bushy mustache, wire-rim pince-nez spectacles—the old-timey ones with a chain and no earpieces—and a vintage suit with a pocket-watch chain dangling from the vest, a toy sheriff's star pinned to one lapel, and a small stuffed teddy bear pinned to the other.

Chief Olaf caught sight of his name on Joe's Keystone Cop badge and growled, "I should arrest you for impersonating an officer."

"Nice costume, Chief!" I said, hoping to deflect his wrath. "President Roosevelt, right?"

The teddy bear—named after the twenty-sixth president of the Unites States, Theodore "Teddy" Roosevelt—gave it away.

Chief Olaf actually cracked a smile and preened his

fake mustache. "Good guess, Frank. But you're wrong." He tapped the toy star. "Not *President* Roosevelt. *Police Commissioner* Roosevelt."

"Hey, your costume is almost as clever as mine!" I said, genuinely impressed with our police chief's knowledge of law enforcement history. "I'd forgotten Teddy Roosevelt ran the New York City police department before he became president in 1901."

"And you gave yourself a promotion too, Commish!" Joe quipped.

The chief sighed. "Just stay out of trouble, okay?"

"Always!" Joe chirped.

Chief Olaf just shook his head and walked away, mumbling to himself, "I'm going to regret not arresting those boys, I know it."

"Wow, Sherlock Holmes, Nancy Drew, Police Commissioner Roosevelt, and Chief Not-Exactly-Olaf all at the same masquerade party," I commented to Joe. "Who knew 'crime solver' would be such a popular Halloween costume?"

The party's host still hadn't made an appearance, so we didn't know what Robert had decided to dress up as yet. Guests continued to arrive for another half hour or so before a trumpet blast filled the hall from somewhere above us.

We looked up along with everyone else to see Percy standing at the top of the tall, twin staircases at the end of the hall.

"That kid's got a diverse skill set," Joe remarked.

"Hear ye! Hear ye! Gather round and behold your gracious host! Guardian of Scotland! Liege of Comic Kingdom! Lord of Castle McGalliard! And Thrower of Magnificent Parties!" Percy shouted, putting the trumpet back to his lips and giving another regal toot. "Sir Robert Braveheart!"

The guy who marched out with a long claymore sword triumphantly raised over his flowing braided locks looked only vaguely like the Sir Robert we knew. He had Robert's features and belly, for sure, but his face was streaked with blue war paint, and his formerly bald dome was hidden under the long brown wig. He wore a traditional Scottish kilt with a matching tartan plaid sash draped across his armored leather breastplate.

"Hey, Robert's dressed as that Scottish warrior dude from that famous old *Braveheart* movie, where all the guys in kilts fought that evil king," said Joe. "Pretty spot-on costume, besides his head still being attached."

"William Wallace," I said, filling in the historical blanks of Joe's movie synopsis. "He led the revolt against the British in the First War of Scottish Independence at the end of the thirteenth century."

"I gotta admit, Robert looks pretty sharp in a kilt," Joe noted.

"Looks like Xephyr did a pretty expert job on his custom sword, too," I said, thinking about the other sword she'd crafted. I gave another look around, hoping to see her among the costumed crowd, but a lot of people were wearing masks, and Xephyr was known to get pretty imaginative with her costumes, so who knew what she was dressed up as.

"Welcome to my castle, boos and ghouls! Are you ready to party like your life depends on it?!" Robert shouted to exuberant cheers from the crowd. Lucky even howled right along.

"Are you going to tell us what was on the missing page of *Sabers and Serpents*?" a voice that sounded a lot like Murph's shouted from somewhere up front.

Robert grinned, pointed his sword in their direction, and winked. "Patience, friends. The night is young, and full of dreadful secrets."

Okay, so Robert's nonanswer wasn't a fully honest disclosure of the facts, but at least he'd kept his word not to lie about knowing what was on the page, for now at least. He still didn't miss a chance to promote the shop, though.

"Post a picture of yourself at the party with the hashtags SirRobertsComicKingdom and SabersAndSerpents, and get ten percent off your next purchase!" he called. "Feel free to explore the castle grounds while you're at it. Just stay away from the doorways marked with yellow caution tape, or the cranky old goblin who roams these ancient halls will steal your soul."

People laughed.

"I'm, er, not really joking about that part," he said nervously. "Seriously, don't go past the yellow tape, please."

"Angus," Frank and I both said at the same time.

Robert cleared his throat and continued. "Now, before the festivities officially commence, I have just one more thing to say." He raised his sword high, pausing for dramatic effect.

"Freedom!" he cried, invoking Wallace's famous last word before going off script to add, "And free candy!"

And that's when the screaming started.

"Look out!" a girl in a pirate costume shouted, pointing up at the lifeless body free-falling from the rafters.

14

JOE

I T TOOK ONLY A SPLIT SECOND FOR REAL HORROR to grip the crowd.

"Everybody back!" I heard the chief yell amid the intensifying screams as the figure plummeted past Robert and hit the floor below him with a horrible splat. Only it wasn't guts 'n' goo that came bursting out of the body.

It was candy!

The "body" exploded on impact, showering hundreds of fun-size candy bars and lollipops all over the floor. Shrieks and gasps instantly turned to nervous giggles and shouts of joy as people descended upon the candy corpse like a horde of sweet-toothed zombies.

Frank picked up a piece of papier-mâché shrapnel. "A Halloween piñata. Didn't see that one coming."

Neither did a handful of crying kids or Chief Teddy Bear Olaf, who was glaring up at Robert. "Not funny, McGalliard," he grumbled.

Robert just winked. "Let the partying commence!"

I watched as a greedy six-foot-tall ghost in a white sheet with holes for the eyes and mouth elbowed a little girl in a baseball uniform out of the way to grab a package of candy corn. The flash of a Chewbacca tattoo on the ghost's forearm gave the ghost's identity away.

"Inkpen is here," I said to Frank. "Robert stole all his customers. Guess he's trying to steal all Robert's candy."

"If Don's here, his son Doug probably is too," Frank observed, looking around. "It would be the first time a lot of his old friends have seen him in a while. He's been pretty antisocial since all the gaming action moved from the Ink Pen to Comic Kingdom."

"We should keep an eye on Inkpen and son, for sure," I replied. "I wouldn't be surprised if the comic shop rivalry somehow plays into the stolen copy of S and S."

A little firefighter, a walking fruit basket, and a Sith Lord pushed past us, trying to get in on the candy action. Our four-legged, candy-loving friend wanted to join them. Frank pulled on Lucky's leash to keep him from jamming his snout in a passing wizard's flowing white robe, apparently trying to get at their candy stash.

"I don't know if it's the Inkpens, but hopefully surveilling someone on our list will help us—" Frank was midsentence when Lucky yanked him forward, causing him to yelp out his final thought. "FIND IT! AIEEEE!" he cried as Lucky dragged him in the direction of the candy scrum, bowling people over as he went.

One of his victims was the shocked wizard. At least I assumed they were shocked. The wizard's wig and beard were so hairy, the ensemble nearly concealed their entire face except the prosthetic nose and their eyes. Not that you could really see their eyes. Super-cool-looking special effects contact lenses turned their eyeballs into miniature galaxies of swirling stars floating in space.

"Sorry!" Frank shouted to the galactically hairy wizard as he tried to reel Lucky in.

The headstrong bloodhound just sniffed at the air and yanked even harder in a new direction. The leash slipped from Frank's hand and Lucky went running through the crowd and disappeared down a long corridor on the far side of the main hall, his tail high in the air and his nose low to the ground.

"Lucky, come back!" Frank pleaded as he took off after his disobedient spectral hound.

I shook my head and sighed. Frank had been hijacked by his costume. I figured I'd let my bro deal with his Lucky problem by himself while I continued to scope out the costumed guests to see if I could identify more of our persons of interest. Inkpen was lurking in a corner, munching on his Halloween loot, but Nancy Drew had slipped out of sight, and we still hadn't caught sight of Don, Xephyr, or Murph.

I was just starting to scan the crowd again when I caught someone lurking at the edge of the corridor, peering after Frank. From behind, the person's costume just looked like a black cloak, but when he turned around to see if anyone was watching him, I saw a living painting staring across the room. A living, screaming painting. I'm not exactly an art historian, but this painting was pretty famous, and I knew from art class at school that it was *The Scream* by an old-time expressionist painter named Edvard Munch. Funny name, but it wasn't a funny painting. It was pretty terrifying, really. The mask captured the abstract face with its wide eyes, little holes for a nose, and screaming O for a mouth pretty well. The lurker's costume even had a set of fake hands grabbing the sides of its mask like the subject in the real painting.

I quickly turned away and pretended to be talking to the confused Statue of Liberty next to me so McScreamy wouldn't know I'd spotted him. It was hard to tell what his expression was under the mask, but I had a hunch Mr. Munch was suspicious, whatever it was. I kept watch out of the corner of my eye until he ducked down the hall after Frank. I pulled out my phone to send Frank a warning about his masked follower, but there didn't seem to be any cell service in the castle. My brother had a tail, which meant there was only one thing for me to do: tail Frank's tail while Frank tailed his dog's tail.

The hallway curved to the right, and I waited until

McScreamy had turned the corner, then headed down the hall after him. I reached the bend just in time to watch him run through an arched doorway. What I found when I got there was a bright yellow strip of caution tape crisscrossing a large, slightly cracked wooden door. I threw caution to the winds, pushed the door open, and stepped under the tape.

Chilly air nipped my cheeks as I did. McScreamy seemed to have vanished into the dark. Lucky and Frank hadn't, though. I was standing atop a steep stone staircase. As I started down it, I could see that it led to a huge outdoor courtyard, presumably connecting the eastern half of the castle—where the party and Angus's tower were located—to the eerily quiet, totally unlit western half. In the dark distance below I could see Lucky's glow-in-the-dark plastic cone bobbing through the night, with Frank's key-chain flashlight bouncing along in pursuit. Who knew Lucky's spectral cone of shame would also come in handy as a runaway-canine locator!

As reliably bad as Lucky's luck seemed to be, it wasn't surprising to see the glowing green cone moving farther away from the party toward the really dangerous-looking side of the castle. It irked me that Frank's tail had disappeared from sight. If he hadn't spotted me already, he easily could once I followed Frank. Leaving my bro alone in a part of the castle we hadn't explored with McScreamy after him wasn't an option, though, so I continued descending the stairs in pursuit anyway.

There was enough moonlight illuminating the steps for me to see my way to the bottom, but then it vanished behind the clouds and I had to turn on my flashlight as well. So much for stealth.

"I'm right behind you, Sherlock!" I called out so he'd know it was me as I ran toward the large stone arch on the other end of the courtyard, leading back inside the castle's lower level. I caught up with Frank before he caught up with Lucky.

"You didn't see a screaming painting run by, did you?" I asked as he shone his light down a wide, dusty hallway filled with creepy, dancing shadows.

He gave me a confused look and pointed his light at a crooked portrait of a medieval maiden. "A glow-in-the-dark dog, yes, but the paintings here look like they haven't moved in a while."

"You picked up an artistically costumed tail when you went after Lucky, but I lost him in the stairwell back at the other end of the castle," I explained.

"Huh, I guess we both got the slip, then," he said, then cupped his hands to his mouth. "Lucky!"

"This place is even bigger on the inside than it looks from the outside, and that's saying something. Where are we anyway?" I asked, sweeping my cell phone's flashlight over the jumbled assortment of boxes, furniture, and ancient antiques piled against the walls. From the looks of it, some of the castle's previous stewards had been hoarders.

Frank shook his head. "More or less west of the party, I think, on the opposite side of the castle from Angus's tower, as far as I can tell. Wherever we are, it doesn't look like anyone's used this wing in a long time. We better find Lucky and get back. I didn't realize babysitting a bloodhound would make effective detecting so difficult."

As if on cue, Lucky let out one of his spectacularly spooky howls.

"It's a good thing I know that's Lucky, otherwise I might think this castle was haunted," I said, following Frank in the howl's direction. "With a voice like that, no wonder Doyle cast a hound as a murderous ghost dog."

We followed Lucky's bark down another set of stairs to an underground hallway, where we found him pawing at a closed door.

"Come on, boy, back to the party," Frank said, grabbing hold of his leash.

Lucky ignored him and kept on scratching at the door. Frank gave him a gentle tug, but Lucky refused to budge and added a plaintive howl for good measure.

"Robert was right about you being stubborn," Frank told Lucky.

"Maybe he knows a shortcut," I offered.

The second I turned the door's creaky knob, Lucky bolted inside. Our flashlights illuminated an open chamber leading to two more passageways, one on either side. There was more junk piled against the walls, with a rusty suit of armor guarding the mouth of each passage. Lucky's tail went up, his plastic-cone-encapsulated nose went down, and he headed straight for one of the suits of armor, dragging Frank behind him.

Lucky leaped up on his hind legs like he had when he first met me and put his paws on the empty knight's armored chest. Only unlike me, the knight didn't fall over; it collapsed in a pile of pieces.

I'd been wrong about the suit of armor being empty. Gazing up at us through the decapitated helmet's open visor were the gaping, empty eye sockets of a human skull.

A NOSE FOR TROUBLE

15

FRANK

I ONLY SAW THE OPEN VISOR FOR A SECOND before Lucky knocked the knight's helm out of the way as he pawed through the pile of armor, but there was no mistaking what was underneath. A skull, and it wasn't the only human remain hidden in the suit of armor either. Bones skittered across the floor, tumbling out of the dismantled armor Lucky was doggedly pushing aside with his nose.

My first thought: this was just another one of Robert's Halloween gags. But then I remembered that we were deep under the castle, way past the caution tape, in a wing that looked like it had been forgotten for decades. How many decades? I didn't know, but whoever's skeleton this was, it wasn't ancient. The tattered remains of blue jeans and a dress shirt clung to

121

some of the bones. I wasn't an expert on eighteenth-century fashion, but I knew they sure didn't have blue jeans.

"This one isn't a piñata, is it?" Joe asked, looking a little ashen.

"It's like Lucky knew it was here," I said, trying to process my shock over the dog's discovery. "He followed his nose down here from all the way across the castle."

"Isn't that what bloodhounds are known for? Their sense of smell?" asked Joe.

"They're famous for it, but they don't just follow random scents. When the police use them to chase a suspect or"—I gulped—"to find cadavers, they have to be given an article of clothing or something with the scent on it first so they know what to track. This skeleton looks like it's been in the suit of armor undisturbed for years. How would he have picked up its scent and why now?"

"Um, I don't think it's the skeleton he was sniffing for," Joe said as Lucky emerged from the pile of armor and bones with an expectant look on his face . . . and a skeletal hand still clutching some torn comic book pages in his mouth.

Lucky dropped the hand at my feet and started bouncing around and whining excitedly.

"It can't be . . . ," I muttered, looking down at the crumpled, badly stained pages of *Sabers & Serpents #1* grasped between the bony fingers.

"The missing pages!" Joe exclaimed. "He could have picked up their scent from the stolen comic!"

Lucky started barking loudly as if to confirm it.

"Shush, calm down, boy," I said, thinking about the mystery guest Joe had spotted tailing me. Lucky stopped barking and started whining and dancing around in place instead.

I looked from the stain-obscured but no less distinctive artwork of Filmore Johnson to the torn piece of oversize, pointy shirt collar still clinging to the skeleton's collarbone. I could tell from photos and movies I'd seen that collars like that hadn't been in fashion since the 1970s—when Filmore Johnson went missing, never to be seen or heard from again.

"I think Lucky's nose may have just helped us solve more than one mystery—" I didn't get to complete the thought.

There was a gasp followed by a clatter as the living embodiment of Edvard Munch's *The Scream* stumbled from the shadows.

"You found it!" the Scream cried.

It didn't take me long to place the walking painting's voice.

"Murph?!"

JOE

THE SCREAM'S VOICE INSTANTLY SOUNDED familiar, but Frank identified it first.

"You're the screaming lurker, Murph?" I asked, unable to hide my disappointment. Murph going AWOL suddenly made a lot more sense, and there's nothing worse than being betrayed by a friend.

"Um, no?" he ask-answered with his mouth hanging wide open. Okay, he was wearing a mask with a screaming face that always had its mouth wide open, so the expression didn't exactly tell me anything.

"Off with the mask, dude," I ordered him.

Sure enough, Murph emerged from behind the mask. Frank and I were both staring daggers at him.

"Um, why are you guys looking at me like that?" he asked meekly.

"Like what?" Frank asked. "You mean like the prime suspect in multiple crimes?"

"I didn't commit any crimes, honest!" he yelped right away, but then he seemed to take a second to think about it. "Well, I mean, not any major ones."

Lucky was running around us in circles, barking up a storm.

"Quiet, Lucky," Frank commanded.

"So you deny stealing Robert's copy of *S and S #1* from Comic Kingdom and then trying to play us for suckers so we'd lead you to the missing pages once you found out your pilfered plunder was incomplete?" I asked, running down the most serious of the crimes that came to mind.

"You guys really think I would do that?" I couldn't tell if the hurt in his voice was real or if he was laying it on for effect.

"I didn't think you'd sneak around behind our backs and try to follow us either," Frank retorted.

"And you're the most intense comic book collector we know, with a pretty obvious obsession with *S and S*," I added. "That's what we call motive."

"I'd never steal a collectible! It's against my code," he declared proudly. "I bought or traded for every single thing in my collection fair and square. I didn't want to steal the comic for myself, I just wanted to find out what was inside it. That missing page is one of the collecting world's biggest mysteries, and I wanted to be the collector who solved it!"

Lucky, who had been dancing around and whining by Frank's side, got impatient and started running around and barking at him again.

"Quiet, Lucky," Frank commanded, but it didn't work this time. He just started barking at me instead.

"Not now, Luck, we're trying to conduct an interrogation," I told him. He didn't listen.

He tried Murph instead, barking his deep bark and looking up at our suspect with big, sad puppy-dog eyes.

"Sorry, big guy, I'm allergic," Murph said, sniffling and rubbing his nose for good measure.

Lucky gave Frank one last try, barking loudly and ramming my brother with his cone, nearly knocking him over.

"Ouch! What's gotten into you?" Frank protested.

Lucky gave one more anxious little bloodhound dance, then ran off out the door back toward the courtyard.

"Lucky, come back!" Frank shouted uselessly.

"We'll find him later. He knows this place better than we do anyway," I said. I shot Murph a glare. "Right now we've got a more important party guest to babysit. And he still hasn't told us anything to prove he wasn't involved in the theft."

"But I'm the one who wanted to help you guys find it!" he insisted.

"True, but you wouldn't be the first crook to try to

deflect suspicion by offering to help an investigation," Frank pointed out.

"I didn't need to steal the comic to find out what was in it, and whoever did ruined my plan!" he said, pouting.

"Which was?" Frank prodded.

"I feel terrible for lying to you guys," he said quietly without meeting our eyes—or answering the question.

"You should feel terrible," I said. "Now stop stalling and start spilling."

"I kind of impersonated the guy from Butterby Auctioneers who promised to pay Robert all that money if he agreed to sell it," Murph admitted.

"You're the phony Wendell Leadbetter?!" Frank asked.

"All I wanted to do was trick Robert into showing us the inside of the comic so I could see if I was right about it being a treasure map," Murph said. "I knew he wouldn't do it without real incentive, so I came up with one he couldn't say no to."

"But then someone stole it first, and you pulled the plug on the operation," I surmised. It would explain why the phony Leadbetter had disappeared after the theft.

"I knew you guys would probably be looking into it," he said. "Fooling Robert is one thing, but I've seen you crack enough cases to know I couldn't get the ruse past you. So I shut down the bogus number and e-mail I'd given Robert."

"What had you planned to do if the comic hadn't been stolen? Robert would have noticed when you were the one who showed up at the party to authenticate it," said Frank.

"I was going to have an older collector friend pretend to be Leadbetter and flash a fake check," Murph explained guiltily. "They looked enough alike from his picture online that I didn't think Robert would know any better, and we'd be able to put him in a costume anyway, since Robert wanted Leadbetter to do the appraisal at the party. I wasn't going to have him take the comic, though. After Robert showed everyone the inside of the comic, he was just going to kind of go to the bathroom and never come back."

He the saw the disappointment in our eyes and looked away in embarrassment. "I didn't think it would do any harm, not really."

"Defrauding Robert isn't doing any harm?" Frank asked incredulously.

"I mean, if he was telling the truth about the comic being complete, then all it would do was confirm how valuable it was," Murph rationalized. "And if he was lying, I figured he kind of deserved it for leading all of us on. I swear I was never going to steal it, though."

Incriminating yourself in a different crime from the one you're suspected of is one way to prove your innocence, I guess. I believed him, though. Murph had shown really (really really) bad judgment, but I didn't think he was a thief, and he didn't have anything to gain from lying about trying to scam Robert. This case was full of deception and a bunch of unsolved mysteries: what happened to Filmore, who scammed Robert, who stole the comic, what was on the missing page, and who sabotaged our tires, to name a few. At least the auction scam was another mystery solved. I also had a hunch it ruled Murph out as our tire saboteur.

"My plan pretty much went out the window once the comic was stolen. But with you guys on the case, I knew you were my best chance to find out what was on that page," Murph said, confirming my theory—he really did want us to solve that part of the case, which meant he didn't have any motivation to threaten us off the investigation. "I figured I was out of the loop when you guys wouldn't tell me what you'd found out. Seemed like following you was my best bet." His eyes landed on the skeletal hand with the wad of torn comic pages and practically started to sparkle. "And I was right!"

Murph lunged for the hand, the allure of comic collecting's holy grail clouding his judgment to the facts that (a) he was still in big trouble, (b) holding a dead person's hand is downright creepy, and (c) . . .

"Don't contaminate the crime scene!" Frank yelled.

But it was too late. The hand came apart, bones dropping to the floor as Murph grabbed the pages and began to carefully separate them.

"The map!" he cried, holding out the crumpled page from the center of the wad.

I noticed the stains right away. The paper was covered with faded reddish-brown blotches. It wasn't the type of thing the average Joe might recognize, but a detective Joe sure would. So would a detective Frank.

"Bloodstains," we both said at the same time.

Murph made the same face his Scream mask had and dropped the map like it was about to bite him.

"From the faded coloring, they're really old ones too," I said.

"Like, 1970s old, if you ask me," Frank said knowingly as he pointed to the large, seriously unstylish old-fogey shirt collar sticking to the dead guy's clavicle. "That's about the last time a collar like that was in vogue."

"Who do we know of who went missing in the 1970s and was known to tear pages out of every copy of *Sabers and Serpents* he could get his hands on?" I asked rhetorically.

"My thoughts exactly," Frank agreed.

"Whoa! You mean this pile of bones is Filmore Johnson?" said Murph, turning a shade greener.

"That's my guess," Frank said. "Somehow Lucky must have picked up the comic's scent and discovered the remains of Filmore still clutching the missing pages from the incomplete copy Robert found."

"It's almost as if he tore the pages from the comic during a violent struggle at the very moment of his death." I shuddered at the thought. I shuddered again at the next one. "And instead of calling the police, someone went to the trouble of dressing the body in an ancient suit of armor to cover it up and left him secretly entombed in a forgotten wing of Angus's castle."

"I think we might have to have another conversation with Angus," Frank said with a gulp. Murph had stopped listening. He was on his hands and knees, staring intently at the map.

"Look at this, you guys!" he said excitedly, snatching it off the floor and flipping it over. It hadn't taken him long to get over his shock at rummaging through Filmore's quite possibly murdered remains. "I was right!"

Frank and I leaned down to look over his shoulders as he turned the map back over to the front side. The right side of the page was too obscured by stains to really read, but on the other half it was easy enough to make out the shape of an island labeled *Lost Isle*, with various landmarks like mountains and villages. Freaky-looking serpents and sea monsters danced in the water off the coast.

"It's a map of an island like Angus told us, but I don't see anything about a treasure," I said.

"That's because we haven't examined the other side of the page yet," Murph said, turning it over gently. His collector's mind seemed to have come back to him.

And there it was. Now the left side of the page was covered by the stains, but the right side showed an illustration of a close-up of the northeast corner of the map, drawn in a different style—while the other side looked like it had been drafted by a cartographer or someone who knew how to professionally draw a map, this one looked like it had been hand sketched.

"This totally matches up with the notes from the smuggler's inventory listed in the 1700s McGalliard shipping ledger that showed up at auction with Filmore's stuff," Murph said enthusiastically.

There was a cove labeled *Loch Raven* toward the top and a small cottage on a round, hilly peninsula overlooking the ocean farther down the coast. The cottage had two defining features: a well, and more amazingly, a windmill—just like Murph had originally predicted. Written above the windmill was the same coded three-letter Gaelic word Murph had shown us before.

This was a treasure map, all right. Only the "spot" wasn't marked with an *X*. It was marked with a windmill and the code word for gold.

17

DISGUISES

FRANK

T HE TREASURE IS REAL!" MURPH EXCLAIMED.
Could Murph have been right all along?
Could the missing map from the make-believe
comic book truly lead to a real treasure? From
the clues we had, the facts added up.

"When we talked to him, Angus confirmed that he and
Filmore copied the map in the comic straight from one that
was tucked inside an old ledger he found in the castle," Joe
said. "It's gotta be the same Paul Magnus ledger Murph
tracked down."

"And the guy who first drew that map meant for it to
lead to eight crates of smuggled gold," Murph insisted. "We
could be holding the directions to a real fortune!"

"According to Angus, that's what Filmore thought too,"

I said, gesturing to the scattered bones at our feet. "Angus dismissed it as fantasy. If he'd taken the time to study the ledger like Murph and Filmore probably did, he'd know it wasn't total nonsense, but that doesn't mean he was entirely wrong about it leading nowhere. Even if it *had* been real at one time, it's still hundreds of years old and shows a Scottish island he said didn't exist on any map."

Joe didn't seem in the least bit discouraged, though. This wouldn't be the first case we'd been on where hidden treasure was involved, and I recognized that look in his eye. He wasn't just in plain old detective mode anymore. He was in treasure-hunter mode.

"But what if Filmore was partially right too? What if it was real, but they were just looking on the wrong side of the ocean?" Joe suggested.

"Whoa. What if it wasn't a Scottish island at all?" said Murph, eyes going wide with the implication of Joe's query.

"PMG would have been running his operation out of Bayport once he immigrated, not Scotland," Joe continued, referring to Angus's and Robert's Colonial merchant ancestor Paul Magnus by his initials.

"Like maybe it could be off the coast of Bayport!" Murph chimed in.

"But there's nowhere around here called the Lost Isle," I pointed out. "And the cove it shows is named 'Loch Raven.' A loch is what they call a lake or a sea inlet in Scotland. You normally wouldn't find that word used to describe a body of water on a map of someplace in America."

"Yeah, but we know PMG was using codes, and he was obviously trying to make the treasure hard to find," Joe theorized. "What if it was just *disguised* as a map of a Scottish island but it was really here?"

"We run right into the same problem Filmore and Angus had when they tried to find it on maps of Scotland," I said, gently turning the map back over to the side that showed the whole island—I was wearing gloves as part of my costume, which not only made preserving evidence easier, but also made holding a dead guy's map a little less icky. "The eastern half of the island is obscured by the stains, but I've studied the geography of the Bayport coast enough on other cases to know there's no island anywhere near Bayport that looks anything like this one."

We'd hit a dead end. All three of us sagged a little.

Joe looked down at the bones still sticking out of the suit of armor. "Well, if it was Angus who, um, knighted Filmore, then we know he was telling the truth about thinking the treasure map was bogus. Otherwise he wouldn't have left it in Filmore's hand when he stuffed him in the suit of armor."

"Something's still not adding up," I agreed. "We pretty much came to the same conclusion Angus did about the map. But what would make Filmore so obsessed with the map that he'd burn down his own business to keep it hidden? Did he just have a breakdown and lose touch with reality entirely?"

"Or did he know something we don't?" asked Joe.

We all fell silent. If there was an answer, it might have gone to the grave with him. I turned the map back over to the close-up of the northeast corner of the island, where the cottage's windmill was marked with the encoded Gaelic word for gold.

There was something about the way the coastline above the cottage curved in the shape of an S, with Loch Raven at the top and the cottage on the peninsula down at the bottom, that seemed familiar. As I looked closer, the shape of the loch started to ring a mental bell too. It took me a second to realize why I recognized them.

"I think you guys are onto something about it being disguised," I said eagerly. "Only, what if it wasn't just a Scottish island disguised as an American one? What if it isn't an island at all?"

Joe and Murph stared at me, trying to put the pieces together for themselves as I studied the map scale drawn at the bottom of the page to help you measure distance.

"Based on the scale, how many miles would you say it is from the loch to the cottage?" I asked.

"Just over two," math-minded Murph said right away.

Just over two. The same distance as it was between two notable landmarks a lot closer to home.

"Loch Raven might make a nice place to put a harbor, don't you think?" I prompted.

I could see the wheels turning in Joe's head.

"What do you notice about the cottage?" I asked.

"It's small?" Murph responded. He didn't get where I was going, but Joe did.

"It's the same distance from the Inner Harbor on a hill overlooking the coastline!" he asserted. "And the windmill tower and the well are next to each other to the structure's right!"

"I want to be excited too!" Murph complained. "Why is the little cottage with the windmill important?"

"They're wearing Halloween costumes," Joe answered enigmatically. "The cottage is really a much larger house in disguise."

"Um, how much larger?" Murph asked, still confused.

"As big as a castle," I said with a smile.

The same thing that must have dawned on Filmore forty years ago had just dawned on us. The island on the map wasn't an island at all—it was a disguised map of Bayport leading to the very castle we were standing in!

AXED 18

LOCH RAVEN IS REALLY THE BAYPORT Inner Harbor, and the cottage on the peninsula is actually Castle McGalliard! Paul Magnus didn't just code the ledger, he coded the map, too!" Murph proclaimed. "Based on the town records, he died in 1774, just a couple months after his last entry in the ledger, so if he had hidden eight crates of gold in the castle and no one else found it, it should still be here!"

"What was that line again in the ledger above the code for gold?" I asked eagerly.

"'Beneath the windmill I lay awaiting, a drop in the bucket and a chain afar,'" Murph recited.

"I bet that's the directions to where the original McG hid

it!" I said. "If the windmill is really the castle's tallest tower in disguise, then it's gotta be under Angus's tower. That's where the symbol for gold is."

"The tower is to the east on the other side of the castle from where we are now," Frank said.

He held the map up against a wooden beam on the wall and took a step back to appraise it from a new angle.

"'A drop in the bucket and a chain afar' must be a riddle, and I bet it tells us the exact spot under the tower where it's hidden," Frank speculated.

"What in the world does 'a chain afar' mean?" I wondered.

Frank's eyes lit up. "Well, 'afar' indicates distance, and it just so happens that a 'chain' was a common measure of length used in the British colonies! They would unfold a sixty-six-foot-long chain to measure land when they were building towns and making maps."

"Um, how did you know that?" I asked. Frank had a pretty good data bank in that noggin of his, but this seemed like a particularly random piece of knowledge.

"Math class," he said proudly. "I saw it in a conversion table in our textbook and asked our teacher why they called it a chain. I knew the things I learned in class would keep coming in handy on cases."

Murph had zoned out and was looking down at Filmore's scattered bones. "Guys, maybe we should tell the police about this."

"We will, but there's no cell phone service in the castle," I said. "So there's not much we can do until we get back upstairs to the party."

"Well, I don't think Filmore is going anywhere," Frank said.

Murph continued to stare at the bones. "Do you think he figured the whole thing out before, um . . . ?"

"There's only one way to find out," I replied, looking around the chamber at the corridors leading off to either side. "I wonder if one of these brings us toward Angus's tower."

The chamber went quiet as we pondered the question, only it didn't stay quiet for long.

THWANG!

SMACK!

I heard the crossbow release before I saw the ancient bolt shoot from the shadows and pin the map to the wall.

Frank yelped in surprise, yanking his hand away.

Murph took his Scream costume to the next level with a terrified shriek.

I lowered my head and started running toward the direction the bolt had come from to try and tackle our assailant before they could reload. I didn't make it far.

POOF!

A smoke bomb landed in the center of the chamber and enveloped me in a hissing cloud of thick gray smoke. I covered my mouth and nose with my shirt and tried to fan the smoke away from my eyes with my hand. What I saw didn't make me feel any better about our predicament.

Another suit of armor appeared in the haze, and this one was running straight at us, swinging a large battle-ax.

THE DARK KNIGHT

19

FRANK

THE ANIMATED SUIT OF ARMOR RUN-
ning through the smoke toward me was like
something from a nightmare. Jet-black, glowing red eyes, curved horns rising from its helm.
What looked like blood was smeared over the
twin blades of its ax.

I sucked in a deep breath as the knight rushed Joe with
the ax raised. It didn't swing, though, just shouldered him
out of the way and rushed me next. No, it wasn't rushing
me! It was rushing the map!

If I'd been thinking rationally, I would have leaped out
of the way. Unarmed, with nothing protecting me but a
wool coat, I didn't stand a chance against the fully armored
knight. Instinct took over, though, and I grabbed the end of

the crossbow bolt now pinning the map to the wall and tried to pry it out before the assailant could reach the map.

The knight jabbed me in the ribs with the butt end of the ax, knocking me aside easily.

A second later he vanished into the smoke, along with a very valuable piece of evidence.

"He's getting away with the map!" I gasped, climbing back to my feet.

The knight had fled and Murph did the same—right out of harm's way and back through the chamber door the way we'd come. Only it turned out someone else was blocking his exit. I heard an *OOF* followed by another Murph scream as a figure tumbled out of the shadows into the smoke-filled chamber. This one was wearing a long robe, a pointy hat, and a big, cockeyed, fake white beard. It was the wizard with the cool costume Lucky had knocked over at the party.

The wizard didn't stop to chat. He bolted down the corridor to the left, his beard coming undone and floating to the floor behind him. I picked myself off the floor with a groan and bolted after him. I'd lost sight of the knight and wasn't about to let the same thing happen with his magical, and now unmasked, lurking accomplice.

The wizard must have known the way, because he didn't bother with a flashlight. I didn't have the same luxury. My little key-chain flashlight didn't cast a very large beam, and the wizard had enough of a head start that I couldn't see him. All I had to follow was the soft patter of his shoes against the stone floor. And then that went silent too.

I had no way of knowing if the wizard had gotten away, or if he was simply lying in wait to ambush me. I'd run off down the corridor without bothering to wait for Joe, and now I was regretting it. I had no backup and no idea where on the western side of the castle I was. And neither did anyone else.

I continued cautiously until the beam of my flashlight revealed a doorway off to the right. I approached slowly, hugging the opposite wall in case the wizard was lurking just out of sight. What I found wasn't an ambush. It was a steep, curving stairwell descending even deeper under the castle.

I couldn't tell if my heart was beating from the chase or from fear, and I was about to head back to find Joe when I heard the groan and clank of metal down below. It went silent a second later, but the sound had given away my quarry's location. If I turned back, the wizard would get away and we might never find out who'd stolen the map. I took a deep breath, shut off my flashlight, and made my way as silently as I could down the steps in the dark, feeling my way along the wall as I went. With a little luck, I'd be the one to surprise him this time.

I knew I was near the bottom when a faint flickering light appeared in the distance. The wizard must have thought he'd gotten away, otherwise he surely would have blown out the light. If I was careful, I might be able to spy on him, or maybe even take him by surprise and apprehend him. I crept silently toward the light, my hand brushing against the wall to guide me through the darkened tunnel, my heart thudding in my chest.

Strange shadows moved across the floor ahead of me, but I couldn't make out what was casting them. I swallowed the urge to run and inched slowly forward.

Bad idea.

There was another creak of metal, only this time it was behind me. I swung around just in time to watch a heavy iron gate drop into place with a massive clang.

I'd walked right into a trap.

I grabbed the rusty iron bars and tried to push the gate open, but it wouldn't budge. There was a muffled groan from deeper in the room behind me. Reluctantly, I flicked on my flashlight, dreading what I might see. I was right to be scared.

I was locked in the castle dungeon. And I wasn't alone.

By the dim light of two candles burning in ancient wall sconces, I could see that I was in the central room of a dungeon that had smaller cells along one wall and what looked suspiciously like medieval interrogation devices on the other. Two of our suspects were tied to chairs with tape over their mouths—one in the main room with me and one locked in one of the individual cells.

"Trick or treat," a voice said from the other side of the gate.

I turned to see a match spark to life, illuminating the face of my captor as he lit another candle. It was just about the last person I expected see in the castle's dungeon, although it probably shouldn't have been.

"I always dreamed of having a real dungeon," Dungeon Master Dennis, still in his wizard robe but minus the beard and pointy hat, said perkily. "Pretty cool, right?"

UNDER THE SURFACE

20

JOE

"COME ON! LET'S GO AFTER HIM!" I'D CALLED to Frank a few minutes earlier as I lifted myself off the floor, grabbed the ancient sword from the pile of armor that had concealed Filmore's corpse, and took off after the map-stealing knight as he disappeared into the smoke in the direction of the right-hand passageway.

Frank must not have heard me amid all the chaos, because he wasn't behind me. Or maybe he was lost like I was. The corridor to the right had taken a series of quick twists and turns. I'd managed to keep up with the knight until he dropped another smoke bomb at an intersection where the tunnels forked. When the smoke cleared, I found myself alone and totally turned around.

Whoever that dark knight was, he was smart. He was costumed from head to toe in black, but not all of it was armor. He'd worn sneakers so I couldn't hear his feet clank against the stone floor. It took me a while to pick up his trail from the prints he left in the dust, and by that time he was probably long gone. I followed anyway. I wasn't sure I could find my way back, and I wasn't about to let our perp get away with the treasure map after everything we'd been through on this case.

The sneakers hadn't been the knight's only smart move. I didn't know how long he'd been spying on us in the chamber with Filmore's corpse, but he hadn't just grabbed the map from us the first chance he got. He'd lain patiently in hiding until we'd decoded most of it for him, too. Frank, Murph, and I had been so excited about our discovery, we'd let our guard down entirely. The knight had another treasure-hunting advantage on me as well: he seemed to know where he was going, while I didn't have a clue. If I had to guess, I'd say the tunnel had been winding me back in the general direction of Angus's tower on the east side of the castle, but I couldn't be sure.

The corridor grew narrower and narrower until it felt like the walls were closing in on me. Then it just ended altogether. At least that's what it looked like. When I got closer, I noticed there was a vertical gap in the wall just wide enough for a person to fit through. Unless you got right up close to it, you'd never know it was there. It looked like it had once been sealed over with stone and mortar, but whatever they'd used to seal it 275 years ago had crumbled away.

When I peered through with my flashlight, all I saw was darkness. Before I had a chance to second-guess myself, I took a deep breath and squeezed inside. Luckily, the wall was only a couple of feet deep, and I popped out into a wider tunnel a few seconds later. It was wider, but definitely not *wide*, and led me on a downhill curving path deeper under the castle.

When I first heard the thump in the distance, it was so soft I thought I'd imagined it. But the closer I got, the louder it grew.

Thump. Thump. Thump. Thump. THUMP.

A dim bluish light appeared in the distance, and I immediately flicked off mine and put it in my pocket. I didn't want to give my position away. I crept forward, gently placing every step so as not to make a sound, my hands gripping the sword tightly.

I soon found myself standing at the mouth of a subterranean chamber roughly half the size of our high school gym. I realized the light I'd seen was actually moonlight seeping into the depths of the castle's underground tunnels from somewhere high above. Moonlight wasn't the only thing seeping into the chamber either. From the steady dripping sound and glistening walls, I had a pretty good hunch where both the light and the water were coming from. The old well that was by the tower. There was no other way I could think of for moonlight to reach that far underground.

And that's when it hit me. The knight had grabbed the map before we'd had a chance to work out the other part of the riddle. *Beneath the windmill I lay awaiting, a drop in the bucket and a chain afar.* We knew "beneath the windmill" was under Angus's tower, and thanks to Frank paying Frank-like attention to every detail in class, we knew "a chain afar" meant sixty-six feet away. And now, thanks to the moonlight and the dampness, I knew "a drop in the bucket" meant the old well.

The treasure was buried under the tower, sixty-six feet away from the well—and the map-stealing dark knight had led me right to it!

It made perfect sense. The knight's ability to ambush us and then confidently make his escape meant he had to know his way around the castle a lot better than we did, and with us onto the treasure as well, he'd headed straight under the tower to try and unearth the gold ASAP, before we discovered either it or him.

Too late, buddy, I thought, stepping quietly inside the chamber.

The knight stood on the other side of the chamber, ankle-deep in a shallow, moonlit pool where some of the water had collected. His helmet was off, but he had his back to me, so I couldn't see his face. Water and wood chips flew as he feverishly tried to hack through the submerged plank floor with his ax. Frank probably could have recited off the top of his head the scientific process explaining exactly how the submerged wooden floor had managed not to rot after all these years, but all I knew was that it hadn't. And that there was a good chance eight crates of gold were hidden underneath.

MISSING THE MAP

21

FRANK

'M REALLY SORRY ABOUT THIS, FRANK," DENNIS said, sounding bizarrely sincere given the current circumstances. "The dungeon master getting to lock his players in a real dungeon is pretty amazing, I gotta admit, but I still wish you guys hadn't blown our cover so we could have left you out of it."

A furious, swirling ball of questions ricocheted around inside my skull as I tried to make sense of our predicament. They'd have to wait, though.

"Whatever trouble you got yourself in, I can try to help you through it, but you have to let us out before someone gets hurt," I told at Dennis calmly, hoping he could still be reasoned with. I turned back to my fellow prisoners.

I focused on Charlene first. Our perpetually cranky,

possibly murderous third dungeon mate Angus was tied to a chair in the central room with me. I figured he could wait a few minutes. Charlene was in one of the smaller stone cells, with a set of bars between us. I pressed myself against the bars and reached through them, stretching my arm as far as I could, hoping to at least remove the tape so she could talk. I strained against the bars until it hurt, my fingers just inches from her, but that was as close as I could get.

"Don't worry, Charlene, I'll get you out of here," I said as confidently as I could, hoping it was a promise I could keep.

I could read the expression in her eyes, though, and it wasn't worry. It was fury. She tried yelling through the tape. I couldn't make any of it out, but I was pretty sure the angry, muffled diatribe was aimed at Dennis, and none of it was complimentary.

"I think she might be as good an investigator as you guys," Dennis said from the other side of the dungeon gate. "I didn't think anyone would see through our alibi. If this were an RPG, I'd award her an inspiration point."

Inspiration points were coins that game masters gave to players when their characters did something exceptional. In a game, you could spend your inspiration point to throw out a bad dice roll and roll a new one. Too bad metaphorical coins given out by masters of real dungeons didn't work the same way. It sounded like Charlene really had been on the verge of cracking the case, not that she could tell me what she'd found out.

"You and Joe get inspiration points too, for finding the map and decoding it for us," Dennis said. "As a game master, I'm really proud of the ingenuity and problem-solving you guys have shown on this quest."

It was maddening how sincere Dennis sounded, and more than a little disturbing.

"We're not role-playing, Dennis," I said, trying to shake some sense into him. "This is real life, not a fantasy quest. Someone's going to get hurt, and when people get hurt in real life, they don't just lose hit points like they do in a game."

"Yeah, that part of it really stinks," Dennis said, frowning guiltily. "You guys kind of have me in a pickle, though. If I let you go, I'll probably go to jail, and I've got way too many games I still want to run to let that happen."

Dennis's logic about staying out of jail may have been twisted, but I suspected he had more crimes on his conscience than just locking us in a dungeon, and his concern about jail time basically confirmed it.

He twisted his lips, forcing his frown upside down as the perkiness returned to his voice.

"So I figure if it's got to go down like this, we might as well all look on the bright side and stay positive, right? And seriously, man, this adventure has given me all kinds of great material for the next Sabers and Serpents campaign I'm planning. How often does a game master get to know more about a game than the guy who invented it?" Dennis nodded toward Angus. "You may have pulled one over on us with that comic, but we knew there was a real treasure."

Dennis kept referring to "we," "us" and "our," and his admission about the map helped confirm that the dark knight was his accomplice. If they'd been the ones to steal the map, then it wasn't hard to guess what else they might have stolen.

"So you locked up Charlene for pegging you and your evil knight friend for robbing Comic Kingdom, but why is Angus here?" I asked, trying to bait him into a confession.

Dennis shrugged noncommittally. "The less you know, probably the better."

I walked closer to Angus. His hands and feet were bound to the chair and he had tape over his mouth as I well. I loosened the straps on Angus's hands and feet so they were a little more comfortable, but I thought better of completely untying a possible murderer until I knew what was going on. Dennis didn't seem dismayed when I went to remove the tape from Angus's mouth.

"He gave us an earful, but he won't talk to you," Dennis said. "We've got too much dirt on him. He's not going to rat himself out. Right, Mr. McG?"

Too much dirt, huh? Was Dennis's dirt as incriminating as the dump-truck load I was about to drop on Angus? I didn't know how long Dennis had been spying on us before the knight grabbed the map, but even if he had heard our theory about the identity of the skeleton in the suit of armor,

Angus still hadn't. And it just might persuade him that silence wasn't the right answer.

"Ouch!" Angus yowled as I pulled the tape off. "Oh, thank you, kind lad. Now if you'd just let an old man free so he can stretch his achy limbs . . ."

"I'm sorry, Mr. McGalliard. I'd like to, but I think we ought to have an honest conversation first," I told him.

"An honest conversation? What are you implying? I never have anything but," he protested, sounding hurt. "I'm a mere victim here. I know nothing of what this hooligan is talking about. I've done nothing wrong. I was minding me own business this afternoon as I always do, when I was kidnapped from me tower for no reason."

"I believe you're a victim of kidnapping, all right, and I plan to help get you out of here, but the 'nothing wrong' and 'no reason' parts I'm not so sure about," I said. I wasn't buying his meek-old-man act.

"Why, I don't know what you're talking about," he claimed innocently.

"Would you know more if I told you my brother and I just ran into Filmore upstairs?" I asked.

Angus's eyes went wide as I continued.

"He was still holding the pages he tore out of the comic the last time he saw you. He didn't look too happy about it either."

"Im-impossible," he stammered, sounding and looking as if he'd just seen a ghost. "No one's seen Filmore since he burned down that warehouse all those years ago."

"Are you sure you didn't see him one more time after that?" I persisted. "Right here in the castle?"

"That's preposterous," he said with a shaky voice.

"Actually, technically it was Lucky who ran into Filmore, or the suit of armor that's been hiding his corpse for the last forty years, to be more precise," I said, rolling my best metaphorical deception check as I did. I had a strong hunch that those bones belonged to Angus's ex-partner, but I couldn't prove it, not without either a DNA test or Angus's help. "The copy of *Sabers and Serpents* that Robert found in your old stuff wasn't just missing the map Filmore tore out. It was also covered in stains, and thanks to Lucky, we know exactly what made them: blood. Lucky must have smelled the stolen comic somewhere else already, because he picked up the scent again at the party and led us straight to the matching bloodstained map that had been torn out of Robert's copy—only it was still clutched in Filmore's hand, where I'm guessing you left it after you killed him."

"That's cold-blooded, man. I'm definitely putting that in my next campaign," Dennis commented, whistling for good measure. "I don't see how that changes anything, though."

"Because I think Angus is going down for killing his Sabers and Serpents partner, and I think he'll go down a lot easier if he turns over the crooks who robbed his nephew's shop, kidnapped a couple of innocent teenagers, and held them captive in a dungeon."

"Don't fall for it, Mr. McG," Dennis said calmly, playing it cool and unconcerned. "He's trying to trick you."

"I didn't kill anyone, and no one can prove otherwise," Angus barked, all traces of the feeble victim he'd pretended to be a few minutes ago now gone.

"Oh, I think there's a good chance we can. Our friend Murph was there too, and he ran to get Chief Olaf from the party upstairs," I said, desperately hoping that really was where Murph had run off to. "If that skeleton is Filmore, the crime lab will confirm it pretty quickly, and that's not all they'll confirm. I'm willing to bet they'll find plenty of your DNA all over Filmore and that suit of armor you crammed him into."

"He's bluffing," Dennis called through the dungeon gate, but this time I could hear the uncertainty in his voice.

"I don't have any idea what you're talking about," Angus responded. I could hear the uncertainty in his as well.

"They're going to catch you either way, Mr. McGalliard," I leveled with him. "Talk to me and help us out of this situation, and I know the chief will go a lot easier on you. The crime you committed was a long time ago, and there might be mitigating circumstances. Filmore did basically burn down your business and your life's dream along with it, so you couldn't have been thinking clearly at the time. Prosecutors and juries can be sympathetic to crimes of passion like that. You know what no one is sympathetic to? Murderers who are also accessories to assault, kidnapping, and false imprisonment of minors. They throw everything in the book at them and lock them up for the long haul. So unless you want to kiss your castle goodbye forever and spend the rest of your life in prison—" I let the thought linger for Angus to fill in the blanks for himself.

If this had been an RPG, that would have been a persuasion roll. And it seemed to be working.

Angus sighed, and it sounded like resignation to me. Dennis must have thought so too.

"Don't you say a word, Mr. McG," he warned nervously.

"Or what? I think Mr. McGalliard is too smart to go down for your crimes as well as his own," I said. "And if you don't like it, why don't you open the dungeon door and do something about it?"

That was what we'd call rolling for intimidation. DM Dennis had talked about looking on the bright side. Well, this time, being locked inside the dungeon actually turned out to be an advantage. We might not be able to get out, but there was nothing Dennis could do to stop Angus from spilling the beans without opening the door and coming in. Dennis was a great game master when it came to tabletop role-playing games, but he wasn't that great at the live-action stuff. I was confident that I could take him in a tussle if it came down to it. He knew it too.

"Crud. Well played, Frank. You outmaneuvered me," Dennis conceded. "You know, I am pretty curious to hear what happened to Filmore too. Did you really murder him and stuff him in a suit of armor, Mr. McG?"

"I didn't mean to do it," Angus confessed softly.

"You put him in a suit of armor by accident?" asked Dennis.

"Not that part, you ninny," Angus said. "It was all because of that blasted map. It was the night after the fire. I was in shock. Me own partner, me friend, had ruined me. There was nothing left. No business, no money, not even a single copy of the comic book for me to replicate or even to memorialize our creation. It was all gone, including Filmore. The police were looking, but they thought he had already left town. I told them about his obsession with that nonsensical old map, and they reasoned he'd burned the warehouse down to keep anyone else from seeing it and had gone off on a delusional errand in search of his own fantastical Treasure Island. If only he had. I was roaming the castle halls late that night, trying to make sense of it all, when I heard a noise. I don't remember what I thought, perhaps that it was a burglar. I can't have imagined Filmore would come back after what he had just done. I grabbed an old dagger from the wall and went to investigate. And there he was, sneaking down under the castle."

"So that's when you stabbed him?" Dennis asked eagerly.

"I only meant to confront him," Angus snapped, but then his voice softened. "To ask why he'd done it. But when he turned around, he was holding the comic. The last surviving copy, I thought, the only one not destroyed by the fire. And it was folded open to that horrible map. He saw me and became frenzied, speaking nonsense about how the treasure was inside the castle and he'd share it all with me, but I couldn't let anyone else know." Angus's voice began to rise.

"I demanded to know why he'd set the warehouse ablaze. Babbled senselessly, he did, about needing more time to decipher the final piece of the code and to excavate the crates before anyone else discovered the secret. He'd cracked it, he said, and now the crates of gold could be ours. I knew there was no code, no crates, but I tried playing along with his delusion. I said we still could have published the comics and just kept people out of the castle until we found the treasure, but it was as if he'd lost touch with reality entirely. He lashed out and blamed *me* for the fire! He screamed that it was my fault for not believing him about the treasure!"

Angus was nearly shaking as he recounted the events of that night.

"Furious, I became. Was this make-believe treasure worth more to him than our dream? More than our friendship? Be his precious treasure real or not, was he so selfish, so greedy that he would burn us out and ruin me entire life just to claim it? I demanded that he give me the copy he was holding so I could at least try to reproduce it. To salvage something from his betrayal. The look in his eyes when I reached for it, the way he shrieked, it was as if me friend Filmore was gone and Gollum had taken his place." Angus looked away as if trying to hide from the memory and took a deep breath.

"He turned to run and began tearing out the map as he had with the other copies. I tried to grab the comic back from him. The struggle lasted only a few seconds. To this day, I can still hear the sounds of the pages ripping free and Filmore's scream. He stumbled to his knees, and when I looked down, he was holding the torn pages in one hand and his wounded side with the other. It was all a blur of rage and confusion. I didn't know if he'd fallen on the dagger accidentally, or—" Angus let the thought trail off into nothing. Dennis and I were both riveted in place, waiting for him to continue.

"He collapsed at me feet and moved no more. Even in death, Filmore's grip on the pages wouldn't release," he went on. "Such was the hold of that accursed fairy-tale map on his greed-addled mind."

Dennis gripped the dungeon bars and glared at Angus.

"That's why you killed Filmore Johnson? Because he was selfish and greedy?" he asked in disbelief. "You better look in the mirror, man. First you lie to me about the comic still having the treasure map, and then you double-cross me and steal the comic back from us so you can keep it for yourself, and you're mad about someone else being selfish? I can't believe you betrayed me twice like that after promising us a share of the treasure. Honestly, I'm glad we locked you down here before I went up to the party to spy on the Hardy boys."

Angus was so lost in the fog of his own memory that he

ignored Dennis's outburst entirely. I didn't, though. Angus's confession had angered Dennis into making his own. He'd as much as admitted to conspiring with Angus to steal Robert's comic and then locking the old guy up for stealing it back from him. The dungeon had suddenly turned into confession central!

Now that I knew Angus had double-crossed him, it wasn't hard to guess why Dennis had been spying on us at the party. Undoubtedly for the same reason Murph had: he hoped our investigation would lead him to the still-unaccounted-for copy of *Sabers & Serpents #1*. Spying had paid off for him, too, just in an unexpected way. The comic Angus had stolen back from Dennis was still missing, but he'd witnessed our discovery of the notorious treasure map.

Dennis and I now both knew the treasure wasn't the fairy tale Angus thought it was—and from the sound of Angus's story, Filmore hadn't merely cracked the treasure's code, he'd been on his way to the tower's underbelly to find it when Angus killed him.

"I don't think greed had anything to do with it, did it, Angus?" I asked, turning from Angus back to Dennis. "He doesn't believe in the treasure, let alone care about it, and he didn't want the comic stolen back from Robert because it's so valuable. He wanted you to steal the comic for him because the bloodstained pages inside are evidence directly linking him to his partner's death."

"When it happened, when Filmore . . ." Angus began

speaking again as if in a daze, before trailing off and starting over. "I did not know what to do. No one would believe it had been an accident. I did not even know for certain. I had already lost Sabers and Serpents and every shilling I had along with it. I wasn't about to lose me freedom, too, not for Filmore, not after what he'd done to me. To *us*. So I hid him and the knife away in a suit of armor in a forgotten part of the castle and tried to forget about him myself. The police had no reason to suspect me. To them, I was still the victim. Outside the castle walls, though, people talked. About the fire and the disappearance and the tragedy of it all. Others whispered words like "revenge" and "murder." So I stopped going outside. Soon the world mostly forgot about Filmore and Sabers and Serpents. If only it had stayed that way."

Angus went silent again, lost in his own thoughts. It wasn't the case Joe and I had originally set out to solve, but I had Angus McGalliard's confession to the killing of Filmore Johnson over forty years ago. I'd been right that it had been a crime of passion and not premeditated, and I believed him that it might have been an accident. But solving the legendary disappearance of comic book artist Filmore Johnson didn't do me much good right now. I was still trapped in a dungeon, and I still needed Angus to help me finish cracking the case on the crimes it had spawned: the theft of the comic from Robert's shop and our current imprisonment by Dungeon Master Dennis.

"But Robert showed up and unwittingly dug up the evidence," I said, prompting Angus to continue.

"Aye, I should have left that no-good nephew of mine to the loan sharks in Scotland," he lamented. "Fans and collectors pestered me now and again over the years, but they were easy enough to shoo away." Angus scowled across the dungeon at Dennis. "It wasn't until this hooligan showed up asking about the copy of *Sabers and Serpents* Robert found that I even remembered having kept it."

"So you two knew each other before the comic was stolen?" I asked, looking from Angus to Dennis.

"I just wanted to find out more about it," Dennis said. "I'd heard about Sabers and Serpents from old-school tabletop gamers, but when Comic Kingdom opened and I got to see the comic and play the game for myself, I got hooked. I wasn't thinking about treasure or if there was a real map or anything; I just loved the fantasy world they'd created. Since Robert wouldn't show us what was on the missing page, I figured I'd go straight to the source. I knew people said Old Man McG wouldn't talk to anyone, but I thought I might be able to persuade him—you know, game master to game master, once he saw how much I appreciated it."

I thought about how flattered Angus had been a few days ago when he'd been holding Joe and me at gunpoint and I'd told him I was a fan. It made sense that if anyone could get the old recluse to talk, it would be a serious fantasy RPG aficionado like Dennis. But I also knew how wily Angus could be, and I knew he wouldn't have bothered if there wasn't an angle he could work.

"I knew even back then that I shouldn't have kept that copy," Angus recriminated himself. "It was just that a single copy of the game manual was all I had left of Sabers and Serpents. I didn't know if any other copies of the comic had survived after the fire, and I couldn't bear the idea of the thing I'd worked so hard for not existing at all. Couldn't bear to look at the blighted thing either, so I buried it in a box somewhere and hid it away with the rest of the castle junk. I couldn't have found it again after all these years if I'd wanted to, and I figured no one else could either. I figured I was safe. But then Robert found a copy of the comic in the castle, and I knew it had to be the same one."

"Which also means you knew about the stains inside and how they got there," I pointed out. "Robert thought the stains in the copy he found were just random blotches and spilled ink, but you knew they came from Filmore's blood. Robert had no idea that he was holding the clue to Filmore Johnson's disappearance. But you did."

"The past was returning to haunt me. I had to get the comic back before anyone else opened it up and started asking questions," Angus confirmed. "Only I ain't left the castle in so long, it would look more than a wee bit suspicious if I did now."

"So you played along with Robert's lie that it was a bank-breaking one-of-a-kind complete copy and got Dennis to steal it for you?" I asked. I had a hunch that was where this was going, but I was still having trouble seeing my former friend DM Dennis as a hired thief.

"Robert's the one who stole it from me first. I was just asking my new young friends to fetch it back for its original owner," Angus corrected defensively.

Dennis snorted. "Oh, the original owner, huh? From the way you just told it, you took that comic out of Filmore's hands right before he died. The way I see it, I have as much a right to that comic as anyone."

"Filmore . . . ," Angus muttered to himself.

"Was the dark knight who attacked us and took the map the same accomplice who helped you rob Comic Kingdom while you were away at the LARP camping trip?" I asked Dennis, trying to reconstruct what had happened the night of the crime.

Dennis threw his hands up. "Don't look at me. I voted against having this conversation."

Charlene kept trying to interject, but all that came out were frustrated mumbles. I felt awful ignoring her, but it was impossible to understand her through the tape, and I didn't have a way to take it off.

"I'm so sorry, Charlene," I said, hoping she'd understand. "I know you're ahead of me on a lot of this stuff, but I can't tell what you're saying."

When I turned back to Angus, there was a faraway look in our dungeon mate's eyes.

"Aye, 'twas a ghostly, dark knight that attacked me as well," he said with a shudder. "The fiend kidnapped me from my tower this afternoon and dragged me down here before Robert got home. Like a monster we might have put in Sabers and Serpents, it were. 'Twas as if"—Angus paused—"as if that devil-horned knight were Filmore himself come back from the dead to haunt me."

LIVE ACTION

22

JOE

MY FIRST INSTINCT WHEN I SAW THE knight was to rush in with my sword and stop the thief from stealing the treasure, but my defeat in last weekend's LARP made me think twice. I fancied myself pretty good with a sword, but from the way my would-be foe was handling his ax as he chopped through the floor, he might be better. Forget the "RP," this was all live action, no role-play in sight. Getting stabbed with a foam weapon that looked real was one thing. The only thing that got hurt was your pride. If that knight whacked me with his ax, it wasn't going to take two hits to knock me out, and no one was going to be tapping me back in to play another round.

The smart thing to do was lie in wait like the knight had

before stealing the map, learn his identity, and wait for a safe opportunity to apprehend him.

I took a step back so he wouldn't see me, being careful not to slip. The stones under my feet weren't submerged in a few inches of water like the sunken wood-plank floor on the other side of the chamber over by the knight, but they were plenty slick. As I slid my foot back, I realized it wasn't just the damp that made it slippery. In the faint pale light, I saw a sheet of paper stuck to the sole of my shoe.

My first thought was that the knight must have accidentally dropped the stolen treasure map. I leaned down to pick the crinkled paper up. It was a map of sorts, all right, but it hadn't come from the comic. There was just enough light for me to make out a simple, hand-drawn floor plan of the castle's layout sketched on drawing-pad paper. The ink had started to fade, but I could tell from the ballpoint pen the artist had used that it couldn't be super old, and I could tell from the way they measured distance in meters instead of feet that they probably weren't American, since most of the rest of the world uses the metric system. My guess was that the floor plan had been drawn by Angus to map the castle after he moved in. Wherever the knight had found it, it explained how he knew his way around the castle so well. Even after Frank, Murph, and I had decoded that the treasure was hidden beneath Angus's tower, I wouldn't have had a clue how to navigate through the tunnels under the castle to find it. The knight had known where to go right away.

I folded the paper as quietly as I could and slipped it into my back pocket. Then I pulled out my cell phone to capture the evidence on video. Only I'd been gripping the sword so tightly with both hands that they were stiff, and the phone slipped through my fingers. I quickly picked it up, hoping the knight didn't notice since the sound of the phone hitting the ground wasn't loud. But it was loud enough.

The knight swung around to face me. The last time I'd seen that face, it had greeted me with a friendly smile. This time it sneered, and the knight charged at me with the ax.

23

FRANK

S O YOU NEVER MET DENNIS'S ACCOMPLICE before he kidnapped you earlier today?" I asked Angus, wondering if the dark knight and the person who'd helped Dennis pull off the Comic Kingdom heist were one and the same.

"Aye, I met him. The night of the robbery, but he was wearing all black clothing and a mask like you suspect a burglar might, and he spoke with an accent that was peculiar to me ears. The only person I deigned to speak to about the comic before that was him." Angus narrowed his eyes at Dennis. "An easy mark, he was."

Dennis cleared his throat conspicuously and grabbed the dungeon keys from their hook on his side of the door, jingling them to remind Angus where he was. Angus ignored him and kept on talking.

"I knew folks be thinking the missing page was a map," he said, looking smugly at Dennis. "This one was eager to believe anything I told him, so I fed him Filmore's fantasy about the treasure being real and said I could find it for us if he brought me the map."

I had to laugh. It fit Angus's MO perfectly: conning people into doing things for him by promising them a fortune that he didn't think really existed. It was a lot like how he had lured Robert to America with a bogus inheritance.

"You forgot to tell him the part where you stole the comic at gunpoint as soon as the glass case was open," Dennis said.

"I can't steal what's already mine," Angus insisted sanctimoniously. "If anyone here did any stealing, it's him." He jutted his chin in Dennis's direction. "Your mate Dennis here got that masked henchman of his to help break into Robert's shop. The masked burglar came to the castle alone rolling a suitcase behind him, about an hour after midnight on the night of the break-in, it were. Met me out back in the stables like I'd arranged, so Robert was sure not to stumble upon us. They planned well, I'll give them that. Came prepared with the proper tools to break open the case protecting me comic, just like I asked. Won't be walking around barefoot in the stables no more with all the wee bits of glass everywhere, but it did the trick."

Glass everywhere, huh? The origin of the cut on Lucky's

tush may not have been the highest-priority mystery in this case, but now I knew how he'd ended up with stitches and a plastic cone.

"Aye, the burglar came prepared, but I had a tool he didn't," Angus continued, a mischievous gleam in his eye. "And he wasn't expecting old Angus to be so quick on the draw. I let him do all the work, and then once the comic were free, I pulled out me blunderbuss and sent them packing!"

"Yeah, because you're a backstabbing crook," Dennis said.

"Me? A crook?" asked Angus innocently. "I didn't break into me nephew's comic shop. Nay, you're the crooks, not me, least that's the way the coppers would have seen it. A rather brilliant plan, if I do say so meself. It's not like you could stroll into the local precinct and say you robbed me nephew's store and I wouldn't give you your pilfered loot back."

Dennis gnashed his teeth in frustration. "Grr, as a game master, I gotta admit you outmaneuvered me, but that doesn't change the fact that you're still a backstabbing crook."

"He came back to the castle to whine about it, he did, but I chased him off easily enough," Angus told me smugly.

"I believe your exact words were, 'I never seen ye before in my life. Now get off me property before I call the coppers on ye fer trespassing, ye miscreant,'" Dennis recalled in a pretty good approximation of Angus's Scottish accent.

"And there weren't nothing ye could do about it neither!" Angus proclaimed.

Dennis smiled and dangled the keys in front of the bars

for him to see. "This is the part of the story where I remind you that you're the one locked in a dungeon, not me."

"As an objective observer, I think it's safe to say that you're both crooks," I commented, hoping to put a stop to their bickering.

"I didn't help steal the comic for the money, in case that's what you're thinking, Frank," Dennis said matter-of-factly. "It was the adventure of it. I spend so much time helping other people have make-believe adventures as a game master, I couldn't turn down the chance to go on a real adventure of my own. I'm a good guy. I'm just chaotic good, I guess."

"So what's the point of keeping Angus locked up? We've already established he couldn't have made good on his deal anyway because the copy was missing the page with the map," I said. "He was just playing you to get you to retrieve the evidence of Filmore's death and keep himself out of prison."

"Kind of ironic given where he is now," Dennis observed, rapping on the bars of the dungeon gate.

"It's not up to you to punish him. Keeping him locked up here is only going to make things worse for you when you get caught," I warned Dennis.

"I'm not keeping him down here to punish him. I kind of like the cranky old guy, to be honest," said Dennis fondly. "Originally, we just put him in here to persuade him to give us the comic so we could get the map. I was down here trying to get it out of him before dressing up and going upstairs to the party to spy on you."

"I ain't hid it, I got rid of it!" Angus cut in. "I already told ye."

"I might believe you if I hadn't found this when I was searching your tower right after we locked you up," Dennis said, pulling a chewed-up piece of the comic book's back cover from inside his wizard's robe. "Lucky had been chewing on it, and I figure if there's one page, the rest of them are probably still somewhere in the castle as well. Not that it matters as much now that we have the map."

I nodded to myself, mentally marking another box on the mystery checklist. Dennis had the torn back cover hidden in his wizard disguise when Lucky ran over him at the party, which explained how my canine sidekick picked up the scent that sent him after the long-lost pages he found hidden in the suit of armor with Filmore's skeleton.

"We would have gone on thinking the comic we stole was a complete copy if it weren't for your detective work, Frank," Dennis continued. "I didn't know Angus was lying about the missing pages until just a little while ago, when I followed Joe to that chamber where you found Filmore and the map. Thanks again for decoding it, by the way."

Dennis looked past me to Angus.

"Turns out the joke's on you, Mr. McG. The treasure is real, and we know how to find it."

"Nonsense," Angus snapped. "You're as delusional as Filmore was if you think that map leads anywhere."

"Oh, not just anywhere," Dennis said. "It leads right under the tower you live in. The Hardy boys figured it out. You've been sleeping right on top of a pile of gold all these years."

"It can't be," Angus muttered in disbelief.

I gave him a reluctant shrug. "We kind of think it could."

Even after everything Angus had done, I couldn't help feeling bad for him. Filmore had obviously been disturbed, but he hadn't been delusional about that map. If Angus had listened to him, Filmore might still be alive and Angus might be wealthy instead of struggling to keep the castle lights on.

"Speaking of the treasure," Dennis interjected, glancing down at his watch. "Wow, time flies when you're living out a fantasy. There's a lot of gold to carry, and I should probably make myself scarce just in case anyone else figures out we're down here. It's been a lot of fun being your dungeon master, and I wish I could keep hanging out, but I've got to run. See you around."

Then he stuffed the keys into his pocket and started to walk away.

"You can't just leave us here!" I shouted. "No one knows we're here, and we don't have any food or water. Someone could get seriously injured or worse!"

He let out a conflicted sigh and came to a stop. "Oh, man. These kinds of choices are a lot easier when you're just role-playing an adventure. The real thing is kind of stressful.

I don't want anything bad to happen to you guys, but if I let you out, you'll just try to capture me. Kind of puts me in a pickle, you know?"

"You're already in deep trouble, Dennis. Don't make it worse," I warned him. "The police will go a lot easier on you if do the right thing and let us go."

"Yeah, that might make sense for the old guy, but my plan involves not getting arrested at all. Running away and starting a new life with a bundle of treasure seems like a better option. Sorry." He turned back down the hall and kept going.

"You're lying to yourself if you still think you're a good guy, Dennis!" I yelled after him. "Only villains leave their friends and the elderly gagged and helpless in a dungeon. You're not chaotic good. You're neutral evil!"

At first it looked he was going to keep walking, but then he hung his head and turned around.

"Man, you're right. This quest has my character align-ment totally out of whack. I just don't know how to do right by both of us at the same time." He suddenly snapped his fingers. "I know!"

He reached into the pocket of his wizard's robe, but the object he pulled out wasn't the key ring like I'd hoped. It was the silver twenty-sided gaming die he carried everywhere. "Tell you what. You can roll for it."

"You want me to roll a D20 to determine whether we possibly live or die?" I asked.

"Yeah. Just like in a game. We let the dice decide. Roll high, something good will happen. Roll low, and, well . . ." Dennis made the thumbs-down sign. "Like I always say, the die don't lie."

"Seems fair to me," Angus said. "You ask me, life often feels like a roll of the dice anyway. At least this way you know the odds ain't rigged."

I turned to Charlene, who gave me an *are you really considering this?* look.

I shrugged, turned back to Dennis, reached through the dungeon gate, and grabbed the D20.

I crouched down to the floor, closed my eyes, and rolled for it. I could hear the metal die clink to a stop on the ancient stones.

"Ooh," Dennis said in that super-suspenseful game-master way he has when a roll is either good or bad but he hasn't told you which yet. I found out when I opened my eyes.

"Critical hit!" I shouted as I soaked in the number 20 staring back at me from the die. "Yes!"

"Way to go, laddie!" Angus cheered.

Dennis looked a bit stunned. "A crit. Wow. Clutch roll, man. I didn't expect that."

I held up the die. "Trade you for the keys."

Dennis pulled a rusty old key from the key ring and handed it to me. He didn't seem in a hurry to run away, though, and when I put the key in the dungeon lock, I understood why.

"Hey, it doesn't work!"

"Oh, it works, just not on the dungeon door," Dennis replied. "I still have the same problem as before. If I let you out, you'll try to catch me. That key will open your friend's cell, though, so you can let her out. Sorry, Charlene! Putting you in there wasn't my idea," he called over my shoulder before continuing. "And I promise I'll give someone a call so they can come get you as soon as we're safely out of the castle with the treasure."

"Dirty trickster," Angus barked.

"Sorry, peeps, thinking on my feet, and this was the best compromise I could come up with," Dennis said as he turned to go. "Good luck with the investigation. Can't wait to read Charlene's story."

"Wait a second. If it wasn't your idea to lock Charlene in the cell, whose was it?" I asked, my detective's brain still churning through all the unanswered questions. "And how did you pull off the Comic Kingdom heist when you were away at the LARP campout at the same time?"

"I gotta jet, so you can guys can discuss that among yourselves," he said. "Thanks for being my prisoners. This has been, like, the most fun ever."

And with that, Dungeon Master Dennis was gone.

MORTAL COMBAT
24

JOE

SUBMIT OR PERISH!" THE UNMASKED KNIGHT screamed, the ax clashing against my sword, sending me stumbling backward.

"Oof," was all I managed to reply, trying my best to keep my grip on the sword as the impact vibrated painfully through my hands.

You know how sometimes you make silly assumptions based on stereotypes about the way you think a certain type of person is supposed to look or act? Well, it's a good way for a detective to get fooled. I'd automatically assumed the terrifying dark knight was a manly macho dude because a lot of pop culture and stuff teaches us to think that super-fierce, ax-wielding medieval knights are supposed to be manly macho dudes. Well, I'm here to tell you that pop culture and stuff is wrong. And if I didn't figure out something fast, I wasn't going to be around much longer to tell anybody anything else, because Xephyr had me seriously outmatched.

"The treasure is mine, Hardy," Xephyr said, another blow from her ax clanking off my sword. "Surrender and I'll let you walk out of here alive." She jabbed the butt end of the ax into my chest, pushing me off-balance. "I might even share a little of it with you."

"And if I decide to turn you in for robbing Comic Kingdom instead?" I wheezed, still trying to catch my wind from that last blow.

"Then the treasure's hiding place becomes your tomb," she said.

Talk about live-action role-playing! This time the ax definitely wasn't made of foam and this definitely wasn't a game. After the last LARP, I'd bragged about wanting all live action, no role-play. Well, I finally got it all right, and I was already ready to give it back. My opponent was still playing a role, though—even as she tried to hack me to pieces—and I wasn't sure she knew how not to. She was even still using one of the strange accents she'd made up for her characters.

"Noble of you to want to uphold the law, inspector, but is your honor worth dying for? You are but a mere squire in combat with a knight and badly outmatched." She gave a flamboyant twirl of her ax to prove it.

"It doesn't have to go down like this, Xephyr." I tried

reasoning with her. "You don't have to play the villain. You can still do the right thing."

She grinned. "Perhaps I'll give some of the gold to charity. But stop before my quest is complete, I will not."

She took another swing with the ax. I narrowly dodged out of the way and darted farther out of reach. I took up a defensive position, backing away as she stalked forward. If I could stay on defense and keep her talking, I might be able to figure a way out of this. Frank and Murph both knew where the treasure was hidden as well, and I had to hope one of them would find their way here before Xephyr did me in.

"I didn't see you upstairs at the party," I said, spitting out the first thing that came to mind to stall her.

"I was entertaining some guests in the dungeon," she said nonchalantly. I wasn't sure which word had me more alarmed, "dungeon" or "guests."

"Um, voluntary guests?" I asked hopefully.

"It probably wasn't their first choice of accommodations," she said.

I gulped.

"We figured you might be involved when we saw that flamberge LARPing sword you made hanging in Robert's shop," I said, before tossing in a compliment to soften her up. "Amazing craftwork, by the way. It looks as good as the real thing."

Xephyr paused her attack to soak in the praise. "I do have a knack for it, don't I?"

"You're a master sword-smith, to be sure," I agreed. "Only problem is, there's no way you could have replicated it without having been in Angus's tower to see the real thing first."

"You're wrong, actually. A friend snapped a photo for me, but it was rather indiscreet of me to reproduce it. It was just so hard for me to resist such a beautiful weapon." She gave her ax another twirl and advanced.

"I was guessing the same friend probably picked up the caltrops and sabotaged our tires?" I asked.

Xephyr grinned in confirmation and took a step closer.

"So how did you and this friend of yours manage to break into Comic Kingdom while you were away on the LARP camping trip?" I continued. If I was going to perish in combat, I might as well solve the mystery while doing it.

"And here I thought the Hardy boys were supposed to be the best detectives around," she mused. "Although I don't expect the school reporter will be telling anyone what she discovered."

"So Charlene really was about to break the case?" I asked, but then the second part of what Xephyr said sank in. "Wait, what do you mean she won't be telling anyone?"

"She came snooping around Angus's tower after the party started, after I had picked the lock on the gate and was inside searching for the map. I was wearing my full suit of armor, but she guessed exactly who I was even with my helmet on. Turns out she'd already seen through my alibi and knew who to look for."

"But we saw the pictures of you LARPing on the Bayport Heights camping trip at almost the exact same time the store was robbed," I said, lunging with my sword to slow her advance while I tried to figure out what Charlene had seen that we hadn't.

"Did you?" she asked as she knocked my blade away with her ax.

I thought I had, but we'd had no reason to be suspicious when we first saw the pictures. We'd taken it for granted that the photos were what they appeared to be and hadn't examined them closely. Another bad assumption that had come back to haunt us, apparently. I recalled the photographs people had posted around the time of the crime. You could see Xephyr's face when her werebear mask was off in some of the earlier shots, but she'd been wearing it in all the midnight ones, so it technically could have been someone else in disguise—but that meant another LARPer must have been in on the ruse to put on her costume after Xephyr had already snuck away to drive back to Bayport and commit the crime. Which also meant it couldn't have been someone who appeared in any of the same late-night pictures at the same time.

"DM Dennis!" I blurted. Her scowl told me that I'd gotten it right. "How did Charlene tell it was really him in the pictures and not you?"

Xephyr took a wild swing for my head, leaving her off-balance. I swatted the ax away with my sword and took a swipe of my own to create more space between us as I backed away.

"It should have worked," she grumbled. "I made sure the costume covered every inch of us from head to toe. Dennis even wore lifts in his shoes so we were the same height and just growled to stay in character when anyone tried talking to him. But he'd been wearing a leather pouch full of dice on his hip for his archer costume, and he put my costume on over it without taking the pouch off first. She saw the lump on his hip in the same place and made the connection. Once she started going back through all the Internet posts and interviewing people from the camping trip, she realized no one had seen or photographed the two of us together for over an hour."

"Huh, I guess Dennis was right. The die don't lie."

Xephyr smiled. "I'll have to tell him that after I take you out and escape with the treasure."

I slashed at the air between us to keep her at bay.

"Makes sense that you were the one to commit the crime, since you knew your way around the shop better than anyone. Well, except Robert," I observed. "And your fingerprints were already all over the place, so the police wouldn't have been suspicious when they dusted the place."

"Dennis devises the plot, I execute the action," she boasted, knocking my sword away with her ax and slicing my Keystone Cop jacket sleeve in the process.

"Has anybody ever told you two that you take role-playing a little too seriously?" I asked.

"All the world's a stage, and all the women and men merely players," she replied with a smile. "I knew the alarm system was just for show, and I could have used my key to walk right in if I wanted. Tampering with the back lock so I could bust in quickly and making it look like a forced entry was Dennis's touch."

"So if you were nosing around in the tower when Charlene ID'd you, where was Angus?" I asked. I knew Mr. McBlunderbuss wasn't about to let anybody near his tower if he could help it.

"He's been a little tied up today," she said with another devious grin. "Charlene cut my search for the map short, but I should probably thank her. I'd already left Dennis at the party to spy and was busy making Charlene at home in the dungeon when I heard Lucky barking. It led me straight to you, Frank, and Murph. And the map, of course."

"And you'd already studied the castle's layout—" I started to speculate about the floor plan I'd found lying on the ground, but a swipe from Xephyr's ax cut the thought short.

"Astute, inspector," she said as I just barely dodged out of the way. "I found a drawing of it among Angus's keepsakes. Once you figured out that the treasure was under the tower, I knew just where to go. I was expecting a little more time to myself, though."

"Sorry to disappoint you, Xeph," I said, parrying another swipe of her ax and forcing her back with my sword.

We'd fought our way back over toward the shallow pool

covering the wood planks Xephyr had been hacking to pieces. I didn't have to pace it off to guess this was exactly sixty-six feet from the well shaft outside the tower. From the looks of the chopped-up floor, Xephyr had been about to break all the way through when I showed up. I could see old crates sitting just below the surface through the cracks.

"Whoa, there's really something there," I told her. I mean, all the clues added up, and I'd known there was a good chance there might be, but to actually realize you were on the verge of uncovering a three-centuries-old treasure kind of took your breath away. It was also really distracting.

When I looked back up, Xephyr's ax was slicing through the air above my head. There's nothing like an ax about to cleave you in two to snap you back to reality. I raised my sword just in time to deflect the blow, but the sheer force of it sent my weapon flying from my hands and skittering across the floor. Xephyr raised the ax again, a fierce scream bellowing from her throat. I dove out of the way just as the ax sliced past me and smashed into the battered plank floor, splintering it into pieces.

I tumbled to the ground and found myself looking straight down at the place where her ax head had landed. Shimmering beneath the water's surface on top of one of the crates were the same three Gaelic letters that appeared by the windmill on the map.

"Gold," I whispered. It didn't look like I'd ever get to see it, though.

Xephyr held her ax straight out in front of her with both arms so it was pointed at my head.

"Bend the knee and bow before me as my loyal subject, and I shall share with you my plunder." Her voice echoed menacingly around the chamber. If she'd been a real knight, Lady Xephyr really would have made a fantastic medieval conqueror. It wasn't the Middle Ages, though, and Hardy boys never bow to crime.

"Sorry, Xephyr, the only lady I serve is justice."

"Then I guess I'll just have to leave you here buried in the treasure's place," she said. And then she raised her ax.

FINAL ENCOUNTER
25

FRANK

TOLD YOU I'D GET THE SCOOP ON THE burglary first," was the first thing that came out of Charlene's mouth as soon as I unlocked the door and pulled off the tape.

I laughed. "I know, you were totally ahead of us."

"You did solve a famous cold case and possibly locate a real treasure, though," she said as I untied her from the chair. "I guess we could've shared information. Next time we can team up, but I still get the exclusive."

"Deal." I grinned. I held out my hand and we shook on it.

"Oh, it's a very sweet reunion. I might even clap if my hands weren't tied up," Angus said, his words dripping with sarcasm. "But we're still locked in a dungeon, in case ya hadn't noticed, and those kids are after my treasure!"

"So it's your treasure now, huh?" I asked. "Until a few minutes ago, you didn't believe it even existed."

"My castle, my treasure," he insisted defiantly. "Now stop your dawdling, and let's go after them."

"And how do you propose we do that?" Charlene asked, pointing to the locked dungeon door.

"I may not have left me tower much these last years, but in my younger days, I did quite a bit of exploring in these halls, and I happen to know there's a secret entrance," he revealed. "If you open the iron maiden in the corner, you'll find a trapdoor that circles back around to the hallway."

Standing in the back corner was a human-shaped iron casket with a lady's face sculpted into it. It looked a bit like the type of sarcophagus you'd find a mummy in.

"Pull open the lid and give the spikes along the top of the maiden's back a tug," Angus instructed. "Mind your fingers, now, laddie."

I did as Angus instructed, cringing at all the nasty-looking spikes lining the inside of the iron maiden, and pulled the ones on top toward me. There was a groan as the spiked back wall of the maiden swung open in response, revealing the doorway behind it.

"What's the quickest way under the tower?" I asked.

"Untie me and I'll lead us there," Angus urged.

"No offense, Angus, but I've heard your knees creak," I pointed out. "Charlene and I will be able to get there a whole lot faster without you."

"I suppose I can follow behind," he relented. "Ain't as spry as I used to be. Ye won't steal my treasure, will ye?"

"Promise," I said.

"Promise," Charlene agreed. "I just want the story."

"Go back to the chamber where you found Filmore and take the other corridor. It'll zigzag and meander easterly, but as long as ye don't turn off the main path, ye won't get lost. Hang a right at the first big fork and keep going. It looks like a dead end, but there's a crack, and a ways beyond that is a leaky chamber next to the old well shaft. It's the lowest point of the castle that I know of. There's another entrance from above, but that's the fastest route from here," he instructed. "Now untie me and let's get a move on!"

"I'm really sorry to do this, Angus, but you've confessed to multiple crimes and you're known to threaten shooting people with a blunderbuss. I'm not sure I trust you running around unsupervised," I said.

"You tricked me!" he shouted.

"We never said we'd untie you," Charlene informed him.

"I promise we'll come back for you as soon as we can," I assured him.

"Don't leave me here!" he cried after us as we exited through the doorway in the iron maiden and took off running for the treasure's hiding place.

When we burst into the chamber, it was already too late.

"Nooooo!" I screamed as Xephyr's ax cut through the air

toward Joe, who lay weaponless on the ground below her, too far away for me to help.

Mine wasn't the only scream to pierce the air, though. A mighty war cry froze Xephyr in place. When she turned, she found Sir Robert Braveheart in his kilt and long, flowing wig rushing toward her with the claymore sword she'd designed raised and ready to strike.

Robert swung, meeting Xephyr's ax midair, only instead of the clang of metal against metal, there was a quiet *swish* as the ax blade sliced clean through Robert's foam sword, severing it in half.

"Uh-oh," Robert murmured.

"So we meet again, Sir Robert," Xephyr spat as Robert backed away, still gripping the claymore's useless foam hilt. "I told you I'd get revenge."

While she was threatening Robert, she wasn't paying attention to Joe. He kicked her leg out from under her, knocking her to her knees, and then he rolled across the ground to grab his fallen sword.

"Here!" he yelled to Robert, sliding the weapon across the stone floor. Robert snatched it from the ground just as Xephyr lifted herself to her feet and raised her ax to strike. Their weapons met in the air again, and this time there was a clang. And another and another as the Bayport Adventurers Guild's two best gladiators faced off in real combat for the first time.

Joe grabbed a wet, splintered board from the smashed-up

planks and joined the fray, whacking Xephyr in her armored ribs. The knight's armor protected her, but the force of the hit knocked her off-balance, giving Robert the advantage.

Charlene and I watched in tense amazement as the costumed warriors clashed, a medieval knight, a Keystone Cop, and William Wallace locked in deadly combat in what had to be one of the most time-bendingly bizarre battles in history.

Xephyr deflected Robert's next blow, then knocked Joe away with an armored elbow and took a one-handed swing at Robert with her other arm. The strike nearly knocked the sword from Robert's hands, but it also left Xephyr with her breastplate exposed.

Joe didn't hesitate. He teed up with the board in both hands and swung it like a baseball bat. It hit her square in the chest.

Xephyr dropped her ax and tumbled backward, splashing into the open hole in the floor and smashing into the crates beneath. She tried to regain her footing, but although the hole only came up to her chest, she seemed stuck, weighed down in the water by her armor.

Charlene and I sprinted toward Joe and Robert from one side while Murph, who must have followed Robert through the other entrance Angus mentioned, sprinted up from the other. The five of us stood over the hole, staring down at Xephyr as she flailed around in the debris. She'd crashed right through the crates, spilling their contents into the water.

It wasn't gold Xephyr was floundering around in, though. It was a few hundred years' worth of thick brown muck.

"Where's the gold?" Murph asked eagerly.

Words slowly materialized beneath the water's surface as a fragment of wood bearing an engraved plaque floated up from the ruined crates. I reached in to pick it up and studied the faded letters. The word "Gold" didn't grab my attention as much as the ones describing it. Everyone was dead silent as I read them aloud.

"'Glasgow Gold, Fine Scottish Tea.'"

The silence continued as we processed it.

"I'd say it's pretty well steeped by now," Robert finally observed, breaking the silence as we all stared down into the muddy water, where Xephyr was still sputtering.

"Looks like you were right about part of it, Murph," I said. "Robert's ancestor Paul Magnus really did hide smuggled goods in the castle to avoid paying taxes to the British Empire."

"Yup," said Joe, picking up where I left off. "It just wasn't gold."

We all looked at Joe as he finished the thought. The ancient treasure that Filmore Johnson had burned down his own business and died at Angus's hands trying to find? That Murph committed fraud because of? That Xephyr and Dennis robbed, sabotaged, and kidnapped for?

"It was plain old fancy Scottish tea."

26

JOE

I'M PRETTY SURE CHIEF OLAF WASN'T EXPECT-
ing our mismatched fellowship of ragged, costumed
adventurers to march back into the party with Xephyr and
Angus in chains.

"We've got a Halloween present for you, Chief!" I
called out as Frank, Charlene, Robert, Murph, and I walked
our prisoners into the main hall, where the chief was busy
assaulting a helpless corn dog. "Sorry for solving the case
without you."

"Whainaworldisgoinonher?!" he said through a mouthful of corn dog, mustard smeared all over his fake Teddy
Roosevelt mustache.

It took us a while to convince him that it wasn't another
Halloween gag and that we really had cracked the Comic

Kingdom burglary case. *And* Filmore Johnson's cold-case disappearance from the 1970s. *And* a super-cold-case missing treasure map mystery from the 1700s.

We conveniently left out the part about Murph conning Robert. Murph had confessed the auction-house scam to Robert on his own and we decided to leave it to them to work out. Not that Robert wasn't mad, but Murph had helped unravel the rest of the case and was going to work off his part in the crime in indentured servitude to Comic Kingdom—Robert had a new job vacancy to fill now that Xephyr was (obviously) fired. Murph had also worked his way back into everybody's good graces by retrieving Robert to help us, and defeating an armored knight in real combat was going to give Sir Rob LARP bragging rights until at least the end of time. And now that we'd recovered the notorious missing pages of *Sabers & Serpents #1*, he could brag about knowing what was on them without lying.

The only parts of the case that had gone unsolved were DM Dennis's whereabouts after he left Frank, Charlene, and Angus locked in the dungeon, and, of course, the location of the stolen comic. Okay, so that was a pretty big one. Angus was still insisting he'd gotten rid of it and was claiming innocence of theft by insisting that Robert had stolen it from him first and you can't steal something someone else stole from you first. There was no shortage of secrets and deception in the McGalliard family, that was for sure.

"I bet that chamber was still dry when Paul Magnus

stashed the smuggled tea there back in 1774," Frank noted as we rehashed what we'd found in the chamber under Angus's tower. "It wouldn't have taken long for that tea to steep into nothing after the well started leaking. But once everything was submerged, the water would have created an anaerobic environment that helped preserve the wood. Otherwise we might not have found anything at all, and the mystery never would have been solved."

Ha! I knew Frank would have a scientific theory for why the wood hadn't rotted!

"That dog of yours has a sharp nose," Chief Olaf complimented Robert when we got to the part about Lucky leading us to Filmore's skeleton and the comic's missing pages. "I worked a canine unit when I was younger, and bloodhounds are amazing creatures."

"He was supposed to be one of your lot, but the coppers rejected him," Robert told him. "All nose, no discipline, they said."

"In this case, I think that lack of discipline may have paid off big-time," the chief said. "From what y'all have told me, when Lucky ran over that Dennis kid at the party, the kid already had the stolen comic's scent on him from the chewed-up page he found in Angus's tower. Sounds like it was chewed up because Lucky already came into contact with it earlier around Angus, and when he smelled it again, it triggered his hunt instinct, and off he went trying to find it."

"That's how we figure it," Frank agreed. "We learned early on in the case that Lucky likes to use important pieces of paper as chew toys. When he tried jamming his nose in Dennis's wizard costume at the party, I'd thought he was going after candy, but now we know it was the torn piece of back cover he'd chewed on earlier. To him it was just a toy."

"It's still odd that he continued chasing the scent of the comic in a new direction after that," Chief Olaf pondered. "Usually there's some kind of verbal command the handler will give to let the dog know it's time to follow a particular scent, but you boys didn't know he'd smelled the comic or what command to give."

"Hold on a second," I said, replaying the incident from the party in my head. Lucky had yanked on the leash right before running over Dennis in his wizard costume, cutting off Frank midsentence just as he said—

"Find it!" Frank interjected before I could finish the thought. "I was talking to Joe about the comic and said I was hoping our surveillance would help us find it, when Lucky pulled me off-balance, causing me to yelp out the last two words."

"That would do it," the chief agreed. "'Find it' is the basic command a lot of trainers use. Lucky didn't know you'd said it by accident."

"Well done, Lucky, my lad, wherever you've run off to this time," Robert said to his absentee dog.

"Normally once a bloodhound finds its target, its handler

gives it a reward as positive reinforcement after a successful run and the chase stops," Chief Olaf expounded expertly, clearly taking pleasure in his expertness. "Since you boys didn't know to give him one, he must have kept on going after he found the comic. Jumping up on a target's chest is what they're trained to do, and from the way you boys describe, that's exactly what he was doing when he bowled over that suit of armor with Filmore Johnson's remains inside it."

"No wonder he went so wild after he found the missing pages. He was expecting us to give him a treat!" Frank said. "The poor guy was barking and bouncing all around and we just ignored him, so he ran off."

"A little bit of praise and a doggie biscuit usually does the trick," the chief said.

"I think we owe him a whole box when we see him again," I said.

Flashing blue and red lights outside alerted us to the arrival of Chief Olaf's backup. Two of his other off-duty deputies had been at the party as well, and they were already waiting outside with Xephyr and Angus.

"Well, I'd better escort our prisoners back to the station and write all this up," Chief Olaf said, grabbing another corn dog for the road and turning back to Robert. "This has been some party, McGalliard, but next year please skip the falling bodies and multiple felony arrests, will ya?"

The chief was almost out the door when we heard Lucky

let out one of his signature creeptastic howls from the direction of the kitchen. Everyone instantly froze in place. If there was one thing this case had taught me, it was this:

"Follow that nose!" I yelled as the five of us and Chief Olaf all took off running.

We found Lucky baying furiously when we reached the kitchen. We also found Dungeon Master Dennis. He was cowering in the corner hiding behind a chair as the big bloodhound barked at him.

"Good boy, Lucky!" Frank called as we piled into the kitchen around the dog and his cornered perp.

Dennis conspicuously slid his hand behind his back as soon as he saw us.

"Oh, um . . . hey, everybody," he said casually as if nothing was wrong.

"Hand it over," Frank demanded, holding out his palm.

"Hand what over?" Dennis asked innocently.

Frank, Charlene, Robert, Murph, Chief Olaf, and I all scowled at him. Lucky growled.

"You know what, dungeon master," Charlene hissed.

He looked like he was about to deny having it, but he must have realized it was useless. "Guess I'm not going to be able to roll my way out of this one, huh?"

Frank and Charlene firmly shook their heads no. He pulled his hand from behind his back, and sure enough, there was Comic Kingdom's stolen copy of *Sabers & Serpents #1*, slightly chewed and missing a back cover.

"My comic!" Robert shouted, quickly plucking it from Dennis's hand.

"My evidence," said Chief Olaf, snatching it from Robert.

"Be careful!" Murph cried, gently taking it from the chief with a tissue and setting it on the table. "You don't touch a comic this rare with your bare hands! Don't you know anything about collecting?"

"Good boy!" Frank gushed, scratching a very happy Lucky behind the ears. Charlene and I both joined in, showering the bloodhound and his amazing crime-solving nose with praise. Chief Olaf even gave him the rest of his corn dog.

"Lucky being so stubborn turned out to be a good thing," Frank said. "He was determined to get his reward for tracking that comic."

By this point, my pretend Chief Olaf costume was a total mess, and Frank's Sherlock and Charlene's Nancy weren't much better off. Chief's Teddy Roosevelt was still in decent shape, but with his mustardy mustache, we made a ridiculously ragged quartet of costumed detectives.

Robert looked at us and started guffawing. "How many detectives does it take to find a rare stolen comic book?"

"Four," I answered. "And one Baskerville hound."

We all joined in laughing. Even Dennis, although his smile faded when Chief Olaf escorted him to the police car.

"We're usually the ones to beat Chief Olaf to solving the crime, and Charlene was determined to beat us," I said. "But the dog out-detected us all!"

"Looks like Lucky beat you to the scoop on this one," Frank said to Charlene.

"I wonder if he'll give me a quote," she said, smiling.

"Now that I have a complete comic, I might just have to do that midnight webcast after all," Robert pondered. "Still a shame about the condition, though."

"I don't know," Murph said. "It doesn't get much rarer than a legendary one-of-kind comic full of bloodstains from an actual crime. When the collecting world finds out about tonight and the real story behind Filmore's disappearance and that map, I bet it could be worth even more than it would be in perfect condition."

I didn't know who technically owned that comic, Robert or Angus, but I had feeling they weren't going to have any more trouble paying Castle McGalliard's bills.